Other novels by Wendy L. Koenig:

Sentient
Insurrection

Birthright
To Be Phoenix
The Last Griffin

Under Twin Suns

Frozen Fire

ONE TO LOSE

Cadillac Press

Cadillac Press
185 Drummond St. Rd
Drummond, NB E3Y 1V9
Canada

2 4 6 8 10 9 7 5 3 1
FIRST EDITION THIS PUBLISHER

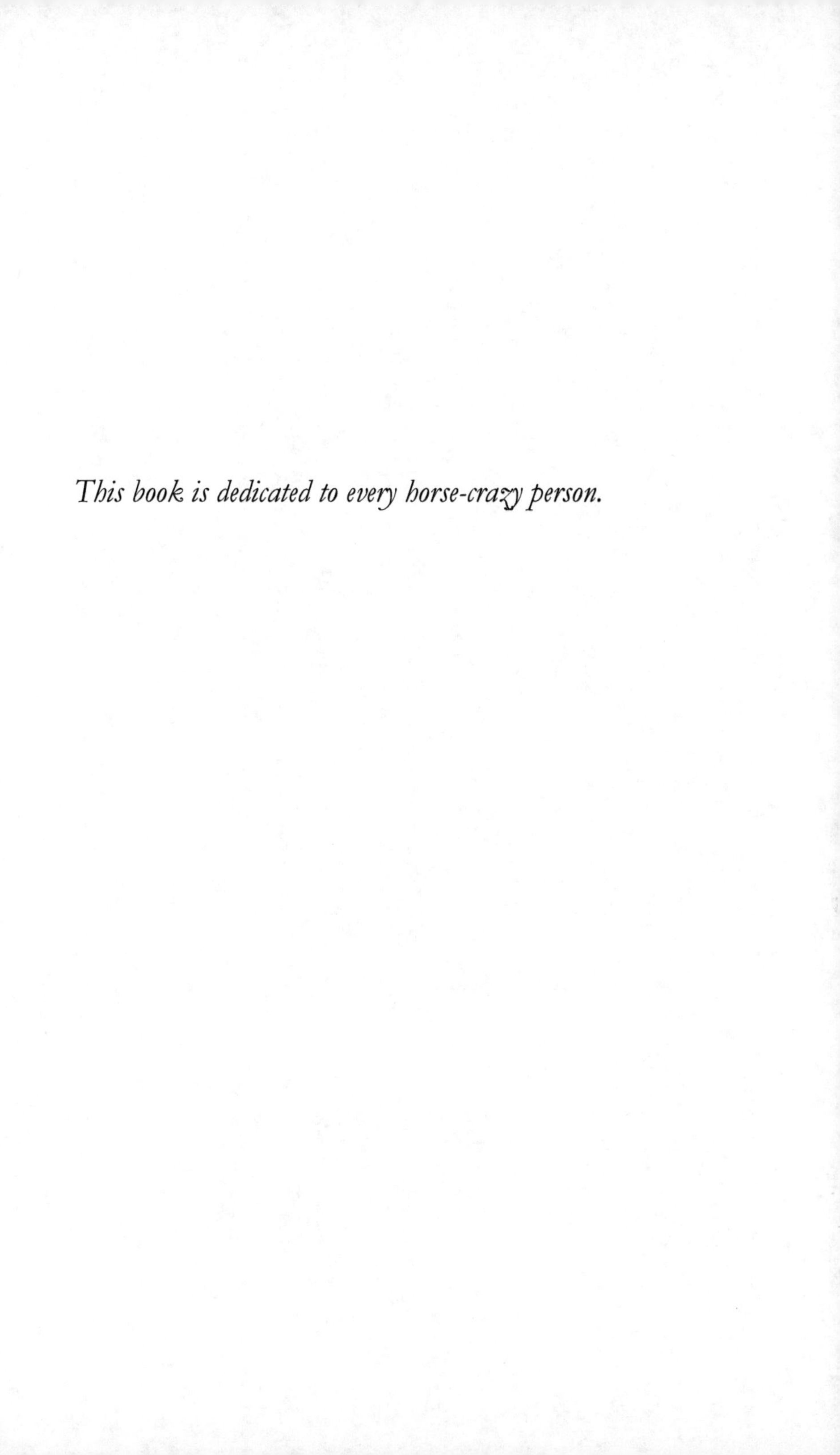

This book is dedicated to every horse-crazy person.

ONE TO LOSE

Wendy L. Koenig

CHAPTER 1

Jesse Marsh stepped off the school bus. Dark storm clouds boiled above the Maine horizon. Just what she needed: more rain. She sputtered her lips in frustration. There were only twenty-seven days till the Aroostook Classic and Jesse still had a lot of work to do with her palomino, Starbuck. He just didn't understand that when Jesse slid her leg back behind the girth, and added the rest of the cues, he shouldn't go forward, but pivot instead. They'd worked on this Turn-on-the-Forehand almost every day for two weeks now, and he still wanted to go forward. Tonight, her best friend Lauren Saucier was coming over to give her a hand.

Jesse dug into her right front jeans pocket for a molasses treat for Starbuck. Her fingers closed on the smooth oblong nugget, and she pulled it out. She held it to her nose, inhaled the deep molasses tang, and smiled. She loved the smell of Starbuck's treats. Behind her, the bus trundled away down the sparse country road.

Only then did she look up at Starbuck's pasture, sweeping her gaze across the grass that swayed in the thick summer wind to the yawning loafing shed. Where was Starbuck? Her palomino always greeted her with a whinny and an exuberant nod. The metal gate of his pasture hung wide open, leaning on the tip. She could have sworn she'd closed it that morning. Now she'd have to go look for him. It would take forever to find him in the woods tonight.

The wind gusted against her, tugging a long tendril of her dark brown hair into her face. She tucked the treat she'd been holding for Starbuck back into her pocket and swiped at her hair. A harsh 'bang' came from the direction of the barn. Adrenaline shot through her, and she jerked her head that direction. The barn door swung back and forth in the wind, flinging back against the wall with another loud crash. Just the wind playing havoc. She laughed at herself and shook her head. Spook.

Tall gray clouds scudded ahead of a dark line above the Maine horizon. It looked like a bad storm coming. The air felt heavy and smelled wet, like rain…again. She'd have to hurry to find Starbuck.

She ran into her and her dad's house and dropped her schoolbag onto their green kitchen table. Maybe her dad had seen the weather and come home early, like last time when he'd saddled Starbuck for her ride with Lauren. In which case, he would have taken Starbuck next door to the Saucier's stable. But then, why hadn't he met her there when the bus stopped to let Lauren off? She tapped her fingernail on the table. Something didn't feel right. He would have let her know if he'd done something with Starbuck. The red light on the answering machine didn't blink at all. No messages.

She reached for her cell phone and called the Saucier's stable, but only got their answering machine. "This is Jesse. If Starbuck is down there, or my father is down there with Starbuck, would you please call back and leave a message? Starbuck might have gotten out of his pasture. I'm going to go look for him. Please tell Lauren. Thanks, bye."

Jesse set the phone down. It might take awhile for the Sauciers to check their messages. She could check if her dad came home early just by calling his office at the Farm and Ag building. She picked up the phone again and punched the third speed dial button. Her father answered on the second ring. That clinched it. "Dad, I guess I left the gate open this morning and Starbuck's gone. I don't know where he is, and no one is answering at Saucier's stable. Can you come home and help me look for him?"

He sighed. "Jess, I'm kinda snowed under here."

"Dad, please! It's getting ready to storm again."

"Alright. Let me organize a few things here, and I'll be on the way. It'll be about fifteen minutes. I'll check Saucier's on my way through."

"Thanks Dad." Jesse hung up. What a time for her to lose Starbuck. Now, she'd have to spend her training time looking for him. She walked down the hallway to go upstairs. Glancing into the living room on her way past, her heart skipped a beat. Books and magazines lay strewn across the floor. The TV stand lay on its side. She stepped into the room. The TV was missing. Her father's trophies, the stereo, the DVD player and the game cube: all missing. Thieves! Starbuck…. Jesse bolted for the barn.

Starbuck couldn't be stolen, he just couldn't be! He had to have wandered away. She'd be able to tell if he'd been taken, the minute she saw her tack room. The thieves would have taken her saddles too. She crossed her fingers, trying to think positively as she ran across the driveway. Her saddles would still be on their perches, and everything would be where it belonged. The wind blustered against her and fought the barn door, shoving it closed twice. The third time, Jesse wedged her leg around the door, holding it open while she slipped inside.

From the door, the tack room looked fine, but as she drew close, she could see that the tack room door had been pried off of its hinges and swung from its padlock. Her horse blankets, sheets and coolers all lay twisted across the floor, brushes and combs strewn on top of them. Jesse's nose stung from the biting odor of the overturned bottles of fly spray and medicine. Dark stains spread across everything. The old halters hung by their ropes, but the hooks where the new halters and bridles had hung were bare. Her old jumping saddle still sat primly on its perch, like it always had, but the new Stubben saddle that her grandparents had given her for Christmas had been taken. Jesse's stomach churned.

The gravel crunched outside the barn and Jesse whirled to face the door, her heart thudding in her chest. There had been no vehicles outside. The thieves had to have left, but who else could it be? Her dad wouldn't be there yet! She backed into Starbuck's empty stall and the deep nest of wood shavings spilled over into her tennis shoes. Jesse crouched low and held her breath.

The door squeaked open, then slammed shut. Shoes scuffed outside the door while the door wrestled open again. A great gust of wind eddied the shavings in the stall Jesse was hiding in. She pinched her nose shut to keep from sneezing. The barn door crashed shut and the only sound was the wind pushing against the barn outside. Then someone sniffed. And coughed. All at once, Lauren's voice echoed from the wooden walls of the barn. "Jesse? Where are you?"

Jesse breathed a sigh of relief. She stood and stepped out of the stall, not bothering to shake her shoes.

"I'm over here."

Lauren rushed forward, her long blonde curls bobbing behind her and the reins from her bridle in her hand. "I got here as soon as I could get Legs saddled! Do you know which way he…?" She stopped when she drew even with the tack room. Her face turned pale beneath her freckles. "Whoa! What happened?"

"Someone broke into our house and my tack room. I…I think they…took Starbuck, too."

Lauren's eyes widened as she stared at Jesse. "No! Have you called the police yet?"

Jesse shook her head. "My phone's in the house. I just discovered what happened. Dad'll be here in a few minutes. He doesn't even know yet."

Lauren held out her cell phone. While speaking to the police, Jesse watched her friend tiptoe past the broken door, into the mess. Lauren turned around and around, shaking her head. Her eyes turned red-rimmed, and she looked ready to cry. Jessie felt numb inside, just like she had when her mother died two years ago. It seemed then as if the world had stopped turning. And now Starbuck….

"Do you think they're still here?" Lauren whispered when Jesse finished with the police.

"No. I don't think so. I just felt spooky. That's why I was hiding when you came."

"Creepy."

"Yeah." Jesse crossed her arms in front of her. Wind gusts boomed against the barn, and she shivered. Her unease grew. The thieves had to be gone. Didn't they? She stared into the shadows behind her and up into the darkened loft. Anyone could be hiding there. "Let's go outside to wait. We can check out the pasture."

Together, they battled the barn door open enough to

wedge through. Heavy gray clouds scudded across the sky, and Lauren's chestnut mare, Legs, grazed in the yard. A roll of thunder echoed through the clouds and the horse snorted and lifted her head. She swiveled her ears in every direction before she put her nose back down to the grass, tearing snatches to chew while she lifted her head and looked around again.

Jesse and Lauren walked over to the pasture gate. The weight of the open steel gate pushed the tip down into deep water-filled tire tracks. Jesse hunkered down on the grass beside them and studied their path.   There were two sets of tracks, one on top of the other. Those hadn't been there that morning. The tracks underneath wobbled.

"Looks like someone backed a trailer up to the gate, and then pulled straight out. Too bad they didn't get stuck." Lauren whispered.

Jesse didn't answer. She tried to swallow the lump growing in her throat, but it didn't disappear.   It grew bigger, almost choking her. They'd taken her Starbuck. He was her life. He couldn't be gone!

The throaty sound of her father's truck filled the yard as he drove up the driveway. Jesse, with Lauren, met him halfway between the barn and the gate. She told him what had happened. At the end, Lauren added, "We already called the police."

His jaw muscles clenched and his dark eyes grew darker. "Girls, I'm going to take a look around. I'll start with the barn."

Jesse nodded. "I don't want to go in there again. I'll wait here."

"Me, too!" Lauren also nodded.

Her father left them for the barn. Neither Jesse nor Lauren said anything.   The thunder rumble had become almost constant now, and had moved straight overhead. The chill wind paused, as if judging the best time for the storm to hit. A blaze of lightning shot across the sky with a sharp crack of thunder right behind. Legs jerked her head up and spooked in great strides, her hips low, like a dog. She stopped her headlong bolt just short of the road.

Lauren turned to Jesse. "I gotta get her home before she goes home without me."

"Be careful."

"I'm really sorry about Starbuck. I'll be back as soon as I can." Lauren hugged Jesse and jogged across the yard toward Legs.

Jesse watched Lauren leave and then faced the barn again. What was taking her father so long? She began to walk to the door when he reappeared. He looked grim and motioned her to wait while he marched off to the house in long tense strides, his head bowed low. By the time he emerged, shaking his head, a Maine State Police car was pulling into the driveway.

"Thanks for coming, Don," Jesse's father said after the officer opened the car door.

Detective Don Lowrey uncurled his legs from under the steering wheel. Then, he stretched one leg out of the car, twisting in his seat to stretch out the other. He stood and straightened his six and a half feet, grinning. "I get all cramped up in there. They just don't make compacts big enough for people like me. Sadly, that's all the department will pay for." He reached to shake Jesse's father's hand. "Hello Ray. What happened?"

Jesse's father told the detective about how Jesse discovered the theft and the tire tracks. The police officer nodded, glancing around at the barn and the gate. He asked Jesse. "Did you touch anything?"

Jesse frowned. "No. I don't think so, and I don't think Lauren did either."

He nodded and pointed to the heavy sky. "I think I'll start with the pasture." Jesse and her father led the way, and the detective followed with a briefcase. He squatted beside the tracks. After several minutes of measuring and drawing in a note pad, he stood and said, "You're right about those being trailer tracks. From the depth, I'd say your horse wasn't the only one in it. Of course, it's hard to tell for sure after all the rain we've had."

As if on cue, small raindrops began to spatter against the ground. They made a hollow metallic 'pling' when they hit the gate. The smell of fresh wet earth and hot pavement filled the air. The detective sighed and examined the gate, dusting places with powder and covering that with tape. He pulled the tape off the gate and stuck it on a card. Jesse leaned in to see. A perfect fingerprint. He grinned at her. "Cool, huh?" After he collected a few more, he asked to see the tack room.

He whistled when he saw the door. "Quite a job." He got out his tape and dusting powder again. After he finished investigating the tack room, they all went to the house to collect information there. Jesse stood at the kitchen window while he filled out his reports. She watched the wall of rain outside and flinched each time the thunder cracked. It seemed to point out Starbuck's absence more. He should be safe and sound in his stall right now, not who knows where, stolen and without her.

Detective Lowrey said, "I'll need you both to come down to the Caribou station to file your prints with us so we can eliminate them. Anybody else we need to eliminate should come down too. Here's my card. You can reach me at that number anytime, it's my pager."

Jesse reached for the card and asked, "Do you think you'll find Starbuck?"

He hesitated, and then answered, "I'm not going to lie to you, trying to recover a stolen horse is tough. We'll have better luck with the electronics. A thief can take a horse and stick him in some back yard and we'd never find him. But, I personally guarantee that we'll do everything in our power to locate him. We'll notify the auction houses and veterinarians nearby, and Border Patrol will keep an eye out, too. I wish I could give you a better promise. I'm sorry."

Jesse's father nodded and hugged her close to him. She leaned her head against his chest. He and the detective spoke a little longer, but she didn't hear the words. A heavy weight settled deep in her stomach. Starbuck was gone!

CHAPTER 2

Jesse opened her eyes the next morning and stared at the ceiling. She resented that the sun sparkled through her window and that happy pigeons cooed on the ledge. First her mother and then Starbuck. Two-thirds of all she cared about was gone. Her heart squeezed tight in her chest and the sting of tears filled her eyes. She sniffed, her lower lip quivering, and tried to rub away her tears with the heel of her hands. Jesse swung her feet out of bed and onto the cool hardwood floor. She walked to the window and pulled the lightweight curtain aside. The pigeons fluttered away.

She fixed her sight on the pasture. The open gate reflected sunlight into her eyes and Jesse squinted to see the puddles that marked the tire tracks. Everything blurred through her tears. She squinched her eyes shut tight and wiped her face again. Tears wouldn't help. They never had, even when that drunk boy had slammed his car into her mom's. He'd broken up with his girlfriend, and though only seventeen, had drunk a full fifth of Southern Comfort. Then that night, he decided to kill himself. Racing near eighty miles per hour, he picked for his mission the first on-coming vehicle he came across: her mom's.

The impact flipped both cars end for end for almost

two hundred feet. He got up and walked away with only a few bruises, while her mom laid in a coma for a week and a half before she died. The boy had been charged with Manslaughter. In a couple years from now, he'll get out of jail and marry the very same girlfriend he'd wanted to kill himself over. His life would go on almost like nothing had happened. Jesse's and her dad's lives had changed forever.

Jesse had spent days then, locked up in her room, staring at the ceiling and sobbing. She refused company, and wouldn't eat the meals her neighbors had brought. There had been no comfort anywhere. Only on Starbuck's wide back had the pain eased to a bearable weight.

What would she do without Starbuck? He was her best friend. Her heart clenched inside her again. She flung herself into her big soft chair, pulling her knees up to her chest and rocking herself. Her tears turned to sobs that shook her until she couldn't breathe.

Her eyes wanted to shut from swelling, and she had a killer headache, but she needed to get to the police station to see if they'd found anything. She dressed and walked downstairs. The living room had been put back in order, and her father was nowhere to be seen.

Jesse opened the back door and heard someone hammering in the barn. As she walked toward the sound, she avoided looking at the empty pasture. It wouldn't help. Her eyes had no tears left anyway. She concentrated on her feet as they moved across the gravel, dislodging little stones as they went. Her legs felt weighted and unattached.

She slipped into the cool dark of the barn. Starbuck's vacant stall beckoned to her, dark in the shadows. It seemed to taunt her. It pointed out his absence. She took a deep shuddering breath, and looked away. This had always been her favorite place, with its earthy animal and sweet hay scents. Now, wet blanket and pine cleaner dominated the barn. "Dad?"

"In here." His voice came from the tack room. She turned that way and saw that the door had a new set of hinges, hidden against the jam. With the door closed, no one would be able to see them or destroy them. Above the door handle, a new deadbolt glinted in the light of the bare bulb in the tack room. Inside, her father had hung all the remaining tack and equipment. He'd stacked and folded clean blankets and placed them onto new shelves. Other blankets hung wet and dripping from nails in the walls.

"Wow."

He put his hands on his hips and surveyed his work, small wrinkles stretching around his eyes. Jesse had always thought that the wrinkles made the tiny gray streaks in his almost black hair stand out more. "Yeah. I put a lock on the gate, too. Next time it won't be so easy for anyone to break in."

Jesse vision blurred with tears again. Next time? What if the police didn't find Starbuck? She didn't want any other horse. Her tears burned her eyes and spilled out onto her cheeks.

Her dad tossed his hammer onto one of the shelves and put his arms around her in a hug. He smelled like sweat and wet horse blankets. "Jess, they'll find him. They have to. That's all there is to it. I won't let them stop until they do."

She nodded and hugged him back, gulping in air between sobs that she'd thought were all gone. "They'd better."

"I called all the local radio stations first thing this morning and they've all promised to run bulletins throughout the day, every day, as long as it takes to recover

Starbuck. The two local newspapers said they'd do the same thing, but that will only be once a week."

Jesse leaned back and stared up at her dad. He'd been busy this morning fixing the tack room and trying to find Starbuck. What had she done? Nothing, but cry and feel sorry for herself. She hadn't done one productive thing towards finding Starbuck. Not one. She felt her face flush. She told herself that things had to change. She wouldn't waste any more valuable time feeling sorry for herself, while she could be looking for Starbuck.

Her dad kissed her on the top of her head. "Come on. Let's get down to the police station. They might have some news."

By the time they got to the Caribou Police Station, Detective Lowrey had left. The clerk, Lauren's cousin, nodded when he saw them enter the three-room building. He ambled around a giant desk in the center of the main room to shake Jesse's hand. "Lauren has already been here with her family. She told me the whole story. I'm awful sorry to hear about your horse, Miss Marsh. We all are. It's hard to lose a pet like that."

He shook his head and sighed. He shoved his hands in his pockets and leaned against the desk. "I had a sister who had a puppy stolen right from her back yard. Broke her heart. Course, the puppy had no value, but just the same, she was close to it. Real close. I don't know if she's ever really gotten over it." He paused for a moment, and then, with a start, seemed to remember he had to take care of business. "We'll do everything we can to help you find your horse, Miss Marsh."

"Thank you." Jesse wanted to scream at him, tell him that Starbuck wasn't just a pet. He was her friend, closer than Lauren, or even her dad. He had a personality.

He spoke to her with his ear wags and his snuffles. Every subtle move of his body told her something. He even let her lie on him in the pasture while he grazed. He listened to her, too. She told all her troubles to him, all her hopes and fears. How could Starbuck be compared to a pet?

"Thank you," her dad said and shook the clerk's hand also. "We appreciate all the help we can get."

The clerk got a thoughtful look on his face. "Have you put an ad in the paper and on the radio, yet? People might see something if they know to pay attention."

Her father answered, "Yes, I called all the local radio stations first thing this morning and they've all promised to run bulletins throughout the day, every day, as long as it takes to recover Starbuck. The two local newspapers said they'd do the same thing, but that will only be once a week."

The clerk nodded, "You might try some further-away papers or radio stations."

"Thank you, we will." Her father looked around as if to make a point.

"Well," the clerk glanced at Jesse, "let's get started with the fingerprints." He led them behind the desk to a small table in the corner. One end of the table held a computer monitor with a sign at the top that said, "This may be your last chance to smile." Beside the sign, a camera faced a piece of pale gray posterboard that hung on the wall. The other end of the table held an ink stamp pad, a box of large index type cards, and a box of packaged towelettes. A roll of flowered paper towels stood nearby. Fingerprints and ink smudges spotted the empty spaces of the table. The whole corner smelled ammonia-like, and when the clerk lifted the lid on the pad, the smell intensified. Jesse crinkled her nose and glanced at her father. He gave her a quick look, but didn't say anything. The clerk gave a grim smile. "We don't have to fingerprint people very often, so the pad gets dry. I had to refill it this morning." He paused, and then said, "Well, Miss Marsh, let's start with you."

Lauren's cousin took an index card from the box and laid it beside the inkpad. Jesse saw that the card had been divided into fourteen boxes, with a place for her name and address at the top. Reaching for her right hand, he rolled her thumb over the ink and then onto the square marked "R thumb" pressing hard. He took each one of her fingers and did the same. When he finished with both hands, he took her left hand, squeezed her four fingers together and pushed them flat down on the inkpad, not rolling this time. Then he pushed her fingers flat down on the card in one of the big boxes marked "Left Four Fingers Taken Simultaneously." After that, he did the same with her other hand. The clerk handed her a towelette and turned to her father.

Jesse's little finger, where she'd bitten off a hangnail, stung from the alcohol on the towelette, and she hurried to wipe it with one of the decorated paper towels. The one she grabbed said 'Petunia' and showed off outlines of the flower. She leaned across the table and studied her fingerprints while she finished cleaning her hands. They looked like just a bunch of lines to her, but some of them had definite patterns. One, her right ring finger, had lines that reminded her of Starbuck's whorls, the ones on his flank where the hair swirled. There was another, "L index", which looked like a layered mountain. The scar she'd gotten on her thumb at camp last year showed up pretty well, too.

When the clerk finished with her father, they thanked him and drove toward home in silence. Jesse wanted to do something to help find Starbuck. But what?

She stared out the window while she thought. Her dad stopped for a traffic light and Jesse found herself facing a telephone pole. Posters and fliers plastered the pole all the way around. Most of them showed pictures of lost pets. She thought about the clerk and how he'd called Starbuck a pet. It gave her an idea. "Dad, I want to make some fliers to put up all over town."

He looked over at her, his eyebrows raised, nodding. "That's a really good idea, Jess. I'll bet Lauren would help, if you asked her. And I can drive you two around to the different locations to post them." He turned his attention back to the road and said, "We can even run one of those in the newspaper. It's bound to catch someone's attention."

Jesse grinned. For the first time, she felt as if she had a hand in looking for Starbuck. She raced upstairs to her room as soon as her dad stopped the truck in their drive and booted up her computer. Scanning through her pictures, she found one of Starbuck and her together in the pasture.

She remembered that day very well. It had been a sunny day last summer and they'd worked hard in the arena all morning. She couldn't remember what they'd been working on, but it didn't matter. Afterward, she'd given him a bath with the garden hose. He'd always loved that, stretching his neck and trying to drink the water. As soon as she'd finished bathing him, she'd had to get her dad to hurry with the camera. Starbuck had just a short magic time between drying and rolling. She was sure he believed that baths always felt best when followed by a roll. The sun had sparkled off his golden coat, and the soft breeze had fluffed his almost white mane and tail. The second photo her dad took, only half a minute later, caught Starbuck already partway down to the ground. She smiled.

Jesse set the photo down when the light from the

window had shifted across her desk. She glanced at her watch and found that she'd lost almost an hour gazing at the photo. She shook her head. This was no time to waste energy on silly daydreams. Jesse titled the flier "Stolen: The most beautiful horse in the world" and queued the printer for 200 copies. She hoped she had enough ink. Downstairs, she got the phone book and began to list all the places where she wanted to place her fliers. She stopped only for lunch and bathroom breaks.

She kept the cordless phone near her wherever she went in the house. Detective Lowrey might call to say he'd found Starbuck. She waited until late that afternoon, after she had finished the list and then went back upstairs and dialed the pager number Detective Lowrey had given her, keying in her return phone number.

The phone beside her jangled a minute later. Jesse picked it up and heard her dad pick up another line downstairs.

"Jesse? This is Detective Don Lowrey. We got the report back on the fingerprints we picked up at your place. I was reviewing it when you called."

"What did you find?" her father asked his voice loud in Jesse's ear.

She held her breath. If they could identify the thieves, they might be able to track down Starbuck's whereabouts. Or at the very least, where to start looking.

"Well, it looks like a lot of the fingerprints came out smudged. We did lift a few nice ones, though. From what we can tell, two men were involved. One is a known criminal, called Mark Banks. He has quite a history: theft, theft, Grand Larceny, theft, assault, theft again, etc., etc...." He paused.

Jesse's father asked, "What about the other one?"

His voice sounded tight.

The detective took a moment to answer. "The other is Banks' cousin, a man by the name of Louis Riperton. He's been in and out of mental institutions and almost killed a guy a couple years ago. He can be a pretty dangerous fellow."

"Have you found them?" Jesse asked. She stood and walked to her window to stare outside.

Again, the detective didn't answer for a moment. Jesse knew the answer before he spoke. "No, not yet," he said. "They have the same address listed. I called the Sheriff near there, but it turned out to be a church. We're doing everything we can to find them."

Jesse hung up, still staring outside. A church. The thieves were smart. Detective Lowrey had said the one man, Riperton, was dangerous. What if he hurt Starbuck? The sharp pain in her heart spread into a deep constant ache and she hugged herself. On the other side of the window, it had begun to rain again, the drops splattering against the glass.

CHAPTER 3

That night Jesse had a nightmare about her mother. In it, her mother paced back and forth in front of the large picture window in the living room. The smell of baking pumpkin pie floated throughout the house. Jesse could see two pies in the oven. Her mother should have been decorating the window for the holidays, but she didn't have any decorations in her hands. She kept throwing her hands up into the air, like she did when she talked to herself, muttering and shaking her head. Her mother paced and then stopped and stared at the front door, as if waiting for someone.

Jesse called out to her, but her mother didn't seem to notice as she began to pace again.

The pumpkin pie smell began to take on a charcoal quality to it as the pies turned black in the oven. Something klunked against the door, jerking Jesse's attention to it. The door flung open and someone stood in the shadowed woods outside. Her mother turned toward the door with an eager smile and held out her arms to hug her visitor. That's when the man stepped inside. A dark haze covered his face, smudging his features. Jesse screamed, but no sound came. She couldn't make her limbs move. Helpless, she could only watch the scene unfold, powerless to stop it. Her heart felt as if it would tear out of her chest in anguish.

Her mother screamed, shrill and ear piercing. She started to run, but the dark man grabbed her by the hair, knocked her down and tied her up. In silence, he ransacked the house, first one room and then another, throwing everything on the floor. He seemed to be searching for something. Jesse couldn't tell what.

While the man worked, her mother pried her fingernails into the knot and untied herself. She bolted into the dark outside. He chased close behind her, yelling obscenities and threats. As he reached out to grab her, Jesse's mom stretched her arms out in front of her, reaching, reaching. Further and further she extended her arms as if trying to grasp something.

Hooves grew in place of her hands, then her legs became horse's legs and the rest of her body followed suit until she became Starbuck. She surged ahead, like the wind. Somehow, he gained on her. He caught her and spun her off her feet. Tears washed down Jesse's face and she found her voice, screaming, "Mom!" A deep brooding haze filled the night as blood sprayed everywhere, neon red in the dark.

Groans of pain laced the air until her mother/Starbuck ceased to exist. Jesse, released from immobility, scoured the ground, but not a trace remained. She dropped to the ground, sobbing, rocking herself. Her mother, gone. Starbuck, gone. The darkness was empty, except for the man's raspy breath. It sounded close in the dark, waiting and getting closer to Jesse.

Jesse jerked herself awake. Her heart hammered in her chest and her breath came in short quick gasps. She'd soaked her pajamas with sweat. Shivers spasmed her body. The clock by her bed read 3:23 am. Standing, she tugged the blanket off the foot of the bed, wrapped it around her and tiptoed down the hall, past her father's room. She reached the bottom of the stairs and turned to go into the living room. The big picture window sat before her, lethal and menacing. The night outside seemed to call her. Scenes from her nightmare traced through her mind. She stepped backwards and pivoted for the kitchen.

Flicking on the light, she sat down next to the table, her back to the wall and facing the kitchen. She tucked her feet up on the chair with her and wrapped the blanket tipi-style around her. Waves of shivers rolled down her body. Maybe she'd caught a cold. She fought her wrist out of the blanket and pressed it to her forehead. It felt a little warm to her, but not a lot. She sniffed and squirmed her arm back into the warmth of her blanket.

The scenes from her nightmare replayed in her head. The man chasing and catching her mom, killing her. She hadn't had a dream about her mom for at least a year now. She turned her head and stared at the dark living room. She could see the window from where she sat. She remembered helping her mom decorate that. They sang carols while they worked. It had been the rule that anyone who didn't sing had to wash the Christmas dinner plates. After her mom died, Jesse and her dad had tried to keep up the tradition. It hadn't felt the same without Mom and the decorations had faded out of their lives.

Another set of shivers ran through her and she turned away. What she needed was tea. She unwrapped her blanket and stood, glancing at the window again. The image of the dark man flashed through her memory. She shook her head at herself. Such a spook. It had only been a dream, that's all. She scuffed across the room to one of the old fashioned metal cabinets to make the tea. When it had heated in the microwave, she shuffled back to her chair and sat down, still scraping a teaspoonful of clover honey around the bottom of the cup.

Jesse set the mug on the table until she got her feet up and had the blanket rewound around her. She brought the mug close underneath her face. The steam roll up onto her skin and into her nose. It made her eyelashes feel heavy and thick. She inhaled deep into her lungs the sweet chamomile-honey scent. When she exhaled, a puff of steam billowed up onto her face, twisting her view of the cabinets. She sniffed. Tea always made her nose run. She loved tea, though. It had always comforted her. Her mom had loved tea, too.

Jesse felt her attention being drawn to the window again. With a sigh, she placed her tea carefully on the table, uncurled herself and got up. She had to do something about that window. At living room doorway, she hesitated. She pulled the blanket around her and stepped forward into the room, looking on either side of the doorway as she did. The world looked dark outside that window. Her nerves felt tight and strung out as she scooched one foot in front of the other. She flitted her eyes back and forth from the window to the door and back again. Jesse heard her breath coming in short quick bursts. It reminded her of the raspy breath at the end of her nightmare. A shiver jolted through her and she stopped, the blanket slipping off her shoulders. She snatched at it and her elbow knocked against a lamp. It fell back to lean against the wall with a soft 'thunk'.

She set the lamp upright, hoping her dad hadn't heard it fall, watching the stairwell for signs of movement. After waiting a few minutes with no sight of her father, she turned back to her task. Jesse took a step forward, licked her lips, and took another step. Her courage failed her when she neared the door. The images from her nightmare stalked her like the guy in it had stalked her mother/Starbuck. He had come right in that door. The three staggered windows at the top of the door showed her the absolute of night. Anything, or anyone, could be out there and she'd never know. Jesse swallowed and reached a tentative hand forward. She found the deadbolt and slid her hand along the cool metal, making sure it was locked. She took a tremulous breath. Half way there. She shifted her hand to the side of the window, her eyes still on the door, groping until she found the cord. Jesse jerked hard on the cord and the drapes flew shut. She blew out a low half-whistle and turned around, dropping her gaze to straighten her blanket again. She laughed out loud at herself. What a spook.

When Jesse brought her head back up, someone stood in the dark ahead of her! Her heart lunged against her chest, and a bolt of adrenalin zinged through her. The vision of the dark man from her nightmare ripped through her and she let out a small screech, jumping back and dumping her blanket on the floor.

Her father spoke. "Easy there! Don't give yourself a heart attack."

Relief washed through Jesse. Only her father. She snapped up her blanket and scowled. "It's you who's gonna give me a heart attack. You shouldn't sneak up on people like that." She stomped past him and returned to her seat in the kitchen.

Laughter shook his voice as he followed her. "I didn't sneak. You were concentrating so hard you didn't hear me. What were you doing?"

The temperature of her tea had edged over to cool. How long had it taken her to cross the living room? She took her mug back to the microwave. "I was…. The window…. Just closing the drapes."

"You looked like you'd seen a ghost."

"Yeah, well, if I die an early death, it's your fault." Jesse groused. She zapped her tea for twenty-five seconds and steam once again lifted above her mug, bathing her face in its warmth. She ignored her father's thoughtful look as he watched her make her way back to her chair and tuck herself in. She knew that look. It meant he'd figured out that she'd had a nightmare. It was just a matter of time before he asked her about it. She'd tell him, but after the scare he gave her, he'd have to work for her answers.

He reached into the cabinets to make his own tea. He'd picked her favorite Looney Toons cup, the one with Marvin the Martian. After a few minutes, when his tea had heated, he came over and sat on the other side of the table from her. He, too, sat with his back on the wall, facing the kitchen. "Do you want to tell me about it?"

"Tell you about what?" she asked into her tea. Chamomile steam bellowed up at her.

"Why you're up." He slurped some tea off the top of his mug.

"I couldn't sleep that's all." Jesse watched him out of the corner of her eye. He stared straight ahead, a frown on his face. His mug had taken on a definite slant. "You're gonna spill it."

He glanced down at his cup and corrected the angle. "Why couldn't you sleep?" Her father turned to face her, setting his cup on the table.

She shrugged. "Dunno."

"Jess." He strung out the vowel of her name in a soft reproving tone. Jesse hated it when he did that.

"What!?!" She flung her free hand out in a questioning gesture, not quite looking at him. Her tea sloshed in her cup and some spilled onto her blanket. She raised the mug to steady it. She didn't expect him to answer. He just kept his gaze on her. She could feel it on the side of her face. It felt like fire. "Fine. I had a nightmare. OK?"

"About your mom?" He asked, his voice soft. He lifted his cup to his mouth, taking a sip, but watching her over the top of it.

Jesse didn't say anything. Why should she? He already knew the answer. The heat from the tea had made her nose run again and she sniffed.

"It's been a long time since you had a nightmare about her. Almost a year I think." He paused and looked around their large kitchen until his gaze settled back on his mug. He clenched it in both hands and stared down at it. "This business with Starbuck has a way of bringing that up again, doesn't it?" His voice sounded old and haggard.

Jesse turned her head to scrutinize him. She remembered all the nights she'd awakened from a nightmare only to find him already in the kitchen. It never occurred to her that he might have had nightmares, too. Suddenly she felt sorry for being angry, for pushing him to make her talk. She softened her voice. "You, too?"

He lifted his head with a laugh and a sheepish grin. "I heard you tiptoe past my door when you woke up."

Jesse's jaw dropped open. "And you let me come downstairs by myself?"

"I thought you might want to be alone a few minutes before I came down." He started chuckling. "When I DID come down, there you were, creeping through the living room, focused on that door and window."

She closed her mouth with a snap. She must have looked hilarious, the way she expected the boogieman to jump out at her any second. She grinned at the picture.

Her father took a sip of tea. His eyes twinkled at her. "So, are you going to tell me why you had to close that drape?"

She stared at him a minute, and then said, "Nope." She twisted her head back to stare at the cabinets and took a drink from her mug. Of course, she'd tell him. She told him everything. He began chuckling again. After a minute, she turned and stuck her tongue out at him.

CHAPTER 4

Early in the afternoon, Jesse and Lauren scrambled out of the truck at the new six-store 'Caribou Plaza'. Jessie scanned the parking lot. It looked like the Sunday afternoon shoppers had just started to arrive. Already, cars crowded the first row of parking spaces in front of most stores. The 'Plaza Café', at the other end of the line of stores, had in its lot a block of cars lined nose to nose. A group of people, still in their church clothes, strolled on the sidewalk, peering in storefront windows. Most everyone in town came out to the Plaza on Sundays. This Sunday, the 'Farm and Rural Supply' store had a Customer Appreciation Sale, complete with popcorn and balloons. Everybody would turn out for that.

Jesse almost felt giddy with excitement as she turned back to the truck. Today, she thought, she'd get news about Starbuck's theft. Surely, someone she'd speak to would have seen something about it. She reached into the cab and grabbed her thick stack of 'Stolen' fliers. She asked her dad, "How many do you want?"

He squinted and stared at the steering wheel, his lips pursed. Jesse watched him tap his fingers as he counted. After a minute, he looked up at her and said, "Why don't you leave me about twenty or twenty-five. If I need more, I'll stop and make copies somewhere."

She nodded and peeled off a small chunk of fliers and tossed them onto the seat. "Good luck."

Lauren slammed the door shut as Jesse stepped back, out of the way, and they both watched as Jesse's father drove off.

Jesse glanced at her friend. "Ready?"

Lauren gave a single nod of her head, her curls bobbing. She rose up on her toes and pirouetted onto the sidewalk in front of the 'Farm and Rural Supply' store. "Ready. I'll take the 'Out' doors. Thank you, very much."

Jesse grinned. She split the pile of fliers between them and went to stand at the 'In' doors. For two and a half hours, Jesse and Lauren handed fliers to anyone who passed. They munched on popcorn that kind farmers brought out to them, and they chatted with sympathetic neighbors and friends. Everyone sympathized with Jesse, but no one had seen Starbuck, or knew anything about the thieves. By the time they ran out of fliers, Jesse felt dull and dark inside again. She'd been so sure she'd find out something today.

"Let's walk along the stores while we're waiting for your dad." Lauren hooked her thumb toward the shops down the sidewalk. She leaned her head that way, too, with her eyes squinted and her mouth curved into a coaxing smile.

Jesse said, "You just want to see the new dress that The Closet has in its window." Her feet felt heavy, and she really didn't want to go anywhere. She just wanted to sit on the sidewalk and wait for her father. Then, she wanted to go home and cry. She'd never get Starbuck back. She knew that, now.

Lauren pivoted on her heel, nodding her head. "Um-hmm. I do. You should, too. The Classic is just a couple weeks away, and you know they always have a party the night before." She wagged her finger. "You might meet a boy there."

Trailing behind, Jesse felt her lip tremble when she said, "I don't think I'm going this year."

Lauren flashed a sharp look Jesse's direction. "You'll get Starbuck back. My cousin, the one who works in the police department, says it's just a matter of time. Starbuck is a flashy horse, it's not like the thieves can hide him very well. The police department even posted bulletins with other police stations within the state."

"The thieves are smart, Lauren. I don't know how, but they've figured out a way to hide him and hide themselves."

"Maybe, but I still think you'll get him back. Look, it's Stacey Michaud." Lauren stopped in front of 'Pet Haven' and waved at a shiny midnight blue SUV. The Escalade made a sharp swerve and pulled up along side them, passenger's side closest.

Stacey lowered the window and leaned out toward them, her long blonde hair hanging down against the side of the vehicle. She smiled, her gaze pinned to Jesse. "Hi guys. What're you doin'?"

"Passing out fliers," Lauren answered as Jesse leaned down to wave at Stacey's mother. Roberta shifted the vehicle into park and leaned close to Stacey.

Stacey turned to Jesse. "That's right. I remember hearing something about Starbuck being stolen. They took you new Stubben, too?"

Jesse nodded. She glanced down the way they'd come. She wanted to get out of there. Where was her father?   Stacey got a thoughtful look on her face and stared somewhere behind Jesse. "I liked that saddle." She focused back on Jesse, her eyes suddenly harder. "They haven't found any clues yet?"

"No, but they're still working on it. And they know who the thieves are."

If anything, Stacey's eyes grew harder. Roberta asked, "Did you have him insured?" Her voice sounded unnaturally high and tight.

Jesse shrugged, "I dunno. I think so."

Stacey nodded. "Good, then you can get yourself a new horse, something better, with more potential. I can help you look, if you like. There's still time before the Classic."

Lauren butted in. "Jeez, Stacey. That's pretty cold."

Stacey glanced over at her, eyebrows raised. "What? Jesse's realistic. She knows Starbuck couldn't have taken her up too many levels. It's probably a good thing he got stolen. Save her some time from fooling around with a half-rate horse."

Roberta snickered.

Jesse clenched her fists and took a step forward. "Stacey–"

Lauren grabbed Jesse by the arm and started pulling her back from the car. She said to Stacey, "Yeah, well, you haven't been able to beat Starbuck yet, Stacey. So, it seems to me that it's you who needs a better horse."

Stacey's eyes flashed and she turned and said something to her mother. The SUV jolted into gear and sped off.

Lauren let go and Jesse spun away. Her hands and arms shook with anger. Tears brimmed in her eyelashes.

"Jesse, I'm sorry. I shouldn't have called her over." Lauren took a deep sigh. "Sometimes, she's such a jerk."

Jesse swiped her eyes and laughed, "You really told

her at the end. You made her mad."

"She'll get over it."

"And if she doesn't?"

Lauren shrugged. "Then I guess she won't be my friend any more. No big loss. I get tired of listening to how wonderful her horse is." She grinned.

Jesse turned to look down at the Farm and Rural Supply to see if her dad had arrived. Still no sign of the truck. As she turned back to Lauren, her attention was caught by a paper taped to the inside of the window of the pet shop. Big bold letters read, "Reward." It showed a picture of a pair of bay horses that looked to be Morgans. She walked toward it, "Lauren, look."

Lauren crowded beside her. "How come we didn't hear about this?"

Jesse pointed to the phone number. "That prefix is Lincoln County, the one right next to my grandpa's."

"Bob Fellum. Do you think the theft of his horses is connected to Starbuck?"

"I don't know, but I'm gonna call them. Got a pen?"

Lauren shook her head, then nudged Jesse and pointed at the "open" sign on the pet store door. "Be right back."

Jesse nodded and glanced down to the Farm and Ranch Supply again. Her dad's truck occupied the parking space closest to the door. He'd probably gone inside looking for her and Lauren.

Lauren came back outside flourishing a stick pen in triumph. "Ta-daah."

"Dad's here." Jesse gestured toward the truck. Lauren craned her neck to see as Jesse turned back to the flier, copying down the phone number on the back of one of the fliers.

She handed the pen back to Lauren and turned to see her dad walk out of the store and look down the sidewalk for her. He waved when he saw her and turned to get the truck. Lauren rejoined Jesse and together they walked to meet the truck half way.

As soon as Jess got home, she tried to call the number, but no one answered. Throughout the evening, as she studied for her Algebra final, every time she found that her eyes had once again lifted from her equations to the flier that held the scribbled phone number, she picked up the phone and tried to call again. Finally, at almost 11 pm, some one answered.

A male voice answered. "Hello?" He sounded in his thirties or forties.

"Hi. Is this Bob Fellum? I, um, saw a flier about stolen horses."

"Yes, this is Bob." He sounded eager.

"Um, my horse was also stolen." Her voice choked off on the last word, remembering Stacey's words. She swallowed, her throat thick. "Have you recovered your horses, yet?"

Bob took a moment to answer, and when it did it was more subdued. "No. We haven't."

Jesse's throat thickened again and she couldn't speak.

He continued, this time his voice was layered with bitterness. "We've pretty much given up on them. The police didn't seem to put much effort into looking."

"When…when were they taken?" She rubbed her eyes as tears formed.

"Over two months ago, now. We came home from work and they were just…gone."

"I'm sorry. Thank you for your time. I hope you

find them."

"Yeah, I'm sorry for you, too. Give me your phone number. If I hear anything, I'll call you. Good luck. Mine are probably dog food by now."

She gave him her cell phone number and hung up, sobbing.

CHAPTER 5

Monday, Jesse had her eighth grade finals. In the middle of her Algebra test, her mind drifted to a crisp and crunchy September day almost two years ago. It had been four months after her mom had died. The woods had beckoned to her with a soft autumn wind. She'd run out to the pasture with a halter and lead, and vaulted onto Starbuck's blonde back. He'd frisked and pranced, making pretend bucks, dancing sideways out the gate and down the dirt road into the woods. Leaves crushed under Starbuck's feet and the warm spice of Fall sank deep into Jesse sighs. It made her arms and legs tingle with the excitement of the ride.

The brush rustled. All at once, a squirrel darted out at them. It chattered and scolded them. Starbuck pricked his ears forward as the little animal came closer. The squirrel tsk-tsked at them. It darted forward, then paused, and then darted forward again. Starbuck took a step back, then another. Before Jesse knew it, she and Starbuck were almost running backwards. She began giggling. A little bitty squirrel intimidated her big bold horse as much as if it had been a moose.

Jesse couldn't contain her laughter anymore, and the

squirrel hesitated. Then it bolted for the nearest tree. Jesse couldn't stop laughing. She laughed until tears ran down her cheeks. Her side began to cramp into a sharp pain that made her catch her breath and lean to that side. Starbuck had stopped, well out of reach of the enraged squirrel's territory. He stood quietly, and flicked his ears back and forth while Jesse slid to the ground. She clutched her side, still giggling. Together, they'd walked toward home. Jesse had limped until her side quit cramping. Starbuck had eyeballed every leaf that rustled. It had felt good to laugh that day. It was the first time she'd really laughed since her mother's funeral.

Jesse jerked her attention back to the classroom as the bell rang to announce the end of the period. Most of the other students had turned in their tests already. Those that hadn't, stood and filed up to the professor's desk, to drop their exam off. She looked down at her test to see an almost blank page. In a fury, she rushed through almost a quarter of the questions before the professor called her name and motioned to bring her test up. Jesse gave a guilt-filled smile as she handed it in, face down.

That evening, the phone rang and Jesse snatched it up. "Hello?"

"Why, hello Jesse. This is Mrs. Pritchard. Is your fa—"

"Hello?" Jesse's father answered downstairs.

"Mr. Marsh? Do you have a moment?"

Jesse hung up. She didn't want to hear Mrs. Prichard tell her father that his daughter had flunked her final. She couldn't stand the thought of the disappointment in his voice. She flopped on her bed and pulled a pillow close to her chest. Her father's strong voice reverberated up the stairs and along the bare wood floor of the hall. She couldn't quite make out what he said, though. He laughed. That, at least was good. After a few minutes he hung up and began the trek up the stairs. A deep sigh escaped his lips just before he appeared at her door.

"I flunked the test, Dad."

He walked in and sat beside her. "Yep. You did." He stared out the window. "I shouldn't have let you take the test, but I honestly didn't think about it. The only time I had to worry about your grades, before, was when your mother died. But you were completely excused from school, then. And when you went back, you still carried straight 'A's." He looked back at her. "I'm sorry, Jess. My fault."

"I was ready for this test. I knew the stuff."

"I know." He sighed again and then smiled at her. "Mrs. Pritchard understood the problem, and she's going to let you retake the test in a couple weeks."

Jesse nodded. "If they don't find Starbuck, I don't think I'll do any better then, either."

He chuckled. "Well, I don't think you could do any worse."

She stared at him and then began to smile. "No, probably not."

"You'll do better." He patted her leg. "But for now, I don't want you to think about Algebra at all. Deal?"

"Deal." She shook his outstretched hand.

"I've been thinking you might want to go visit your Grandma and Grampa."

Jesse shook her head. "I want to stay here. Detective Lowrey might find Starbuck. Or at least a clue. Maybe I could help him if I was here."

Her father hesitated. "I don't know, Jess. I think it'll do you good to get away."

“I don’t want to get away.”

He flicked his eyes over her face. He smiled and said softly, “Think about it, okay?”

Jesse nodded, but she knew she wouldn’t change her mind.

That evening, after dinner, Jesse and her father sat together in silence on the porch steps. The sun had burned away the clouds without a drop of rain since Saturday. The air puffed soft and sweet, and rippled the grass in the empty pasture, like waves in a puddle. It all looked wrong to her. Starbuck should be there, standing in the middle of the pasture, in that last ray of sunshine that he’d follow as it shifted across the pasture. She closed her eyes and she could still see him. In her mind, for a few moments, he stood in that pasture still, like a golden statue. Her breath caught in her throat. What if they never found him? What was she going to do without him?

She heard a brief clattering on the driveway and opened her eyes. Lauren and Legs trotted across the yard toward them. Lauren rode bareback. Her long legs dangled and bounced against the horse’s side, and her blond curls bobbed in all directions. She lifted her reins for a stop when she reached the porch. "Hi! Any news from Detective Lowrey?"

"No, not since Saturday," Jesse answered. She tried to smile at her friend, but it didn’t feel like a smile. Nothing felt like a smile. Nothing felt right. She didn’t even feel like Jesse anymore. She sighed.

“Maybe you should call him again.” Lauren leaned back and flung her calf over Legs’ withers, sitting one-legged Indian style. Legs fussed and jingled her bit, mouthed it and bumped it against her teeth. “It’s been five days now, and you still don’t have any news.”

Jesse shook her head. "I just don't want to bother Detective Lowrey again. Every second he's on the phone with me, he isn't out looking for Starbuck." She glanced at her father as he nodded. When she tried to look at Lauren again, she couldn't quite meet her gaze. It hurt so much, and she thought maybe she would cry again. She didn't want to do that. She was so tired of crying.

Lauren watched her a moment, and then jumped down from Legs' back. She threw the reins to Jesse and said, "Maybe Legs can help make you feel better."

"You never let anyone even sit on Legs!"

"I know, but you're my friend and I know you'll be good to her."

Jesse's throat tightened, and she knew if she spoke, she would start crying. To sit on another horse right now felt wrong. She didn't want another horse, not even to sit on for a few minutes. She wanted Starbuck. She swallowed hard, and when she finally did speak, her voice sounded husky. "Thanks, but I don't feel too good right now."

"Yeah, I guess I know how you feel. After we sold my first pony I felt sick for a long time. I couldn't eat or anything, and I cried all the time." Lauren sat beside her on the stairs. Legs plunged her nose into the short grass and ripped out huge mouthfuls; roots and dirt stuck out of the corners of her lips while she chewed.

"I remember." Jesse nodded. She frowned hard, and pushed the tears way down inside. It might be the same for her. She might never get Starbuck back. She didn't want to think about that right now.

For a long time, none of them said anything. The horizon turned from a silver-blue to an orange-charcoal. Barn owls began to call their night hunt song, and the air began to crisp. The security lights hummed as their globes flickered on.

Then her father spoke, "Jesse, I'm taking you and Lauren to go visit your grandma and grandpa tomorrow. I've already spoken to Lauren's parents, and they think it's a good idea."

Jesse glanced at her friend. Lauren gave a thumb's up signal. They'd always had fun at the farm. Normally, she'd jump at the chance to spend time on their farm chasing chickens and milking cows. She'd even driven the syrup wagon hitched with Somerset County's most famous residents: the two old mules, Bill and Nattie.

Some of her happiest memories came from that farm. Jesse loved her mother's parents, and it had been ages since she'd seen them. They didn't live very far away, but since her mom died, she'd only seen them twice. Right now, though, all she wanted to do was sit by the phone. She shook her head. "Dad, I told you, I don't want to go right now. Detective Lowrey might find Starbuck, and Lauren's got to get ready for the show."

Her father answered softly, "Jesse, there's nothing you can do here. And if I know Lauren, then I can safely say that Legs needs a break, too. You're going. No argument. I promise I'll call you if anything happens."

CHAPTER 6

They arrived at the farm in Jackman late the next morning, and both of Jesse's grandparents ran out of their tiny house to hug her. Worry lines stretched across her grandmother's face, aging her beyond what Jesse remembered. A wisp of escaped gray hair straggled across her grandmother's face. That hair had once been a deep, rich brown like Jesse's and Jesse's mother's. Her grandmother's dark eyes looked deeper, and sadder than Jesse had ever seen them. She gave her grandmother a long hug, holding on till her grandmother pulled back. She opened her mouth to speak, but the rims of her eyes turned red and she shook her head.

"We been worried 'bout ya." Jesse's grandfather twisted her around, and she saw the same look as her grandmother's echoed there. His eyes dwelt on her face, as if he were trying to guess her thoughts. He wrapped her in a giant bear hug, stroking her hair. Then he straightened, his hand dropping to her shoulder, and reached for her father's hand with the other. "Ray. Good to see ya. Been awhile."

"Yeah. It has."

They shook hands and Jesse's grandfather winked at her father. He turned and grinned at Lauren, patting Jesse's shoulder. "Got somethin' to show you two." He turned her around and pointed out into the pasture. Drying clumps of cut grass dotted the field between thick bright green patches. Dandelions freckled the green everywhere. The mules, Bill and Nattie, munched nose to nose in the center of the pasture. In a darker patch, a second pair of mules grazed beside them. "Got 'em last month. That darned Gil Miller bid against me and popped the price way high. But just when I thought I'd walk away, he quit and the gavel slammed."

Jesse and Lauren walked over to the fence. Lauren stretched out her hand, and kissed at the mules. All four lifted their heads at once and regarded their visitors. Then Bill and Nattie shuffled toward them, with the other two trailing behind. The two new mules almost matched each other in size as well as Bill and Nattie matched, but the newcomers towered higher. And they were colored lighter, almost sorrel, rather than the chocolate brown of the other two. One had a stripe on its face, while the other had a little snip between its nostrils. They looked young, not so thick necked as Bill and Nattie.

"What are they're names?" Jesse asked.

"Well, that's Quervo," he motioned to the one with the stripe and the other's Senorita. I think they're about 3 or so. They don't know how to pull yet. That'll be your job, you two, to help me settle them into the feel of the straps. This afternoon, we'll get them a harness set at the tack auction in Moose River."

Jesse's father lifted his hands. "You'll have to count me out. I've got to get back. I've got mountains of work to do." He kissed Jesse on the cheek and unloaded her and Lauren's matching hunter motif suitcases.

"You sure, Ray? Won't be the same without ya."

Her grandfather took the suitcases and headed toward the house.

Her father shook his head. "Have fun, though. I'd love to be there." He climbed back into his truck and rolled down the driveway to the road.

When his truck disappeared around a bend, Jesse's grandmother said, "Come on inside, and I'll get us some lunch."

"We could eat at the auction." Lauren's voice lilted in a breathless, hopeful way.

Jesse's grandpa laughed as he came back and nodded. "Let's get goin' then."

He, Jesse and Lauren piled into the truck and within an hour they bounced into the parking lot of the sale barn. A cloud of dust fogged around them as they came to a stop.

"Charlie Youman told me last week that he'd seen a couple pair of harnesses go for real cheap here last month." Her Grandpa said, jumping out of the truck. He took long strides toward the sale barn, puffing as he spoke. "Gotta get there in time…to look over the stuff before…the sale starts." Jesse and Lauren half-jogged beside him.

Jesse stopped at the door to stare at all the long tables piled high with boxes, bags, junk and assorted tack and equipment. She'd never seen so much leather in one place in all her life! She inhaled the familiar musty, oil flavor, and grinned at Lauren, who rolled her eyes with a big smile on her face, mouthing an exaggerated "Yummy". She turned and pushed through the crowd toward at a table off to the side filled with bridles.

Jesse loved leather; there was something warm and life-like to it, as if the animal that first wore it had left part of its soul behind. She stepped up to the closest table and caressed a strap. The smooth silkiness on one side of it contrasted with the roughness on the other side. No cracks traced across the leather. She curled it around her finger, and the brown turned lighter, but not white. Nice. Someone had taken care of this piece and had kept it oiled. She lifted her eyes to see her grandpa across from her. He picked up and pulled straps out from under the great piles on top of the table.

Jesse scanned the crowds for Lauren, and saw a couple tables bowed from the weight of saddles in all shapes and sizes. She wandered over and poked at one or two saddles lying nearest to her. One, an Aussie, had polished scrolled silver plates on the billet flaps. Stunning. That was her one regret about Dressage and Jumping: no silver. She sighed. She supposed she'd need a new saddle, if she were ever going to ride again.

A lump formed in her throat and refused to leave. She swallowed hard and shook her head. She wouldn't feel sorry for herself. She wouldn't ask herself how she could ever ride again if they couldn't find Starbuck? And she absolutely would not ask herself that if they didn't find him, how would she bring herself to love another horse? She would concentrate on the leather instead. She patted the nearest saddle, and rubbed her hand across the swell of the seat. Pretty saddle. Smooth leather. If she concentrated hard enough, then she might not cry.

The lump in Jesse's throat grew and her eyes burned. She whirled to find the bathroom before the tears flooded down her cheeks. The crowd cleared for a moment, and she bolted forward. Then she stopped. Lauren had moved near her and was staring at a Stubben saddle on top of the table in front of her.

"Jesse, do you see what I see?" Lauren whispered.

Jesse's stomach did a flip-flop. She lunged across

the table and snatched the saddle from under the scrutiny of a prospective buyer who 'humphed' and stormed away. She flipped it over and over. It looked like her stolen show saddle.

Lauren pointed. "See, there's the scratch it got the first day you put it on Starbuck and he rolled in it."

"Uh-huh." Jesse nodded. She'd been so heartbroken about the blemish he'd put on her brand-new show saddle. It had to be hers, she knew it. Jesse looked underneath. Her father had insisted she engrave her name on the underside of the saddle. She hadn't wanted to mark her new saddle then, but now she was glad she had. "And here's the tops of my J and M. Someone's tried to scratch over my name, but it's still there." Her hands shook, if her saddle was here, then maybe Starbuck was here also!

She whipped her head around from side to side. The horses should be through the door behind the podium. She hugged the saddle close to her, and started toward the stage.

"Jesse, what are you doing?"

"I've got to find Starbuck."

Lauren's hand clamped her arm, and twisted Jesse around. "Yeah, but first we gotta find your Grandpa. He can help us."

"Fine. You go find him and I'll go find Starbuck." Jesse shoved her saddle into Lauren's arms. "No way am I going to lose Starbuck if there's a chance he's here." The crowd swelled, and someone bumped Jesse, pushing her away from Lauren. As she turned toward the podium again, her grandfather materialized from the side.

"Well, there you are. I found a real nice harness over there hidden under a bunch of junk in a box. Don't look! I'm afraid someone else'll notice and then bid against me. Looks like you two found somthin' too. Lets see it."

He reached for her saddle, and then glanced at her.

"Jess, this here looks like your other saddle."

"I know Grandpa, this IS my saddle. See here?" She showed him the scratched out name.

"Honey, I think we'd better go find the manager."

"Starbuck might be here, I need to go check the paddocks." Again, she started toward the door behind the stage, but her grandfather stopped her this time.

He shook his head. "Nope. The sale hasn't started. If he's here, he's not goin' anywhere yet. At any rate, I think we'll be needin' the police."

Jesse glanced her eyes to Lauren, but her friend wouldn't meet her gaze.

CHAPTER 7

The office turned out to be no bigger than Jesse's closet. Two desks occupied the majority of the room, and formed a barricade between the customers and the two older women who seemed too hefty for the room. Spider-web cracks inched across the walls and escaped under the framed poster of a bouquet of flowers in a vase on a red checked tablecloth. The smell of freshly made buttered popcorn permeated the room. Jesse could see the empty bag in a trashcan beside one of the desks.

Jesse and her grandfather both crowded into the space in front of the desks, but Lauren had to wait in the hallway. There were no windows, but a door with its own frosted window adorned the adjacent wall. "Mike Hewell" was painted on the glass.

"We need to speak to the manager," Jesse's grandfather began. Neither woman said a word, and the one with a beehive hairdo returned to her paperwork. The other stared at Jesse's grandfather, but still didn't speak. Her grandfather flushed, cleared his throat and started again. "This saddle was stolen from us, and we can prove it."

The staring woman raised her eyebrows at him. She shook her head and said, "Have a seat in the hallway."

Then she stood, leaned across her desk and rapped on the "Mike Hewell" door. Jesse and her grandfather joined Lauren in the hallway. Together, they sat down on the hardwood bench to wait. For some reason, the woman had made Jesse feel guilty. Maybe the woman had thought she was trying to steal the saddle. She supposed some people would try to scam the auction company. Just like some people would steal a horse.

Someone on the podium tapped the head of the auctioneer's microphone. "Test. One. Two. Test." The volume of the crowd hushed a moment, and then swelled to a greater pitch. Groups of people migrated toward the bleachers.

"You the folks with the stolen saddle?" A tall thin man filled the office doorway, smiling at them. Jesse nodded as her grandfather stood. They followed the man back through the office into the inner sanctum of "Mike Hewell". Diplomas, certificates, photos and newspaper articles littered every available space of the paneled wall behind the mammoth oak desk. The desk itself had its own battle with mountains of papers. A giant black coffee cup with the word "Boss" balanced on the edge of the desk. Paper-covered filing cabinets lined the opposite wall. The single undressed window looked out on all the cars parked for the sale.

Jesse's grandfather shook Mr. Hewell's hand, and, as they all took their seats, recounted the story of the stolen saddle and Starbuck. Mr. Hewell punctuated the story with an occasional question or a nod of his dark head. When the telling had stopped, the auction manager stroked his mustache and said, "Well, we don't really have any security. Most people who come here are real honest. We'll have to call the police." He reached for the phone.

Jesse dug into her pocket and pulled out the card Detective Lowrey had given her. The edges of the card had browned and creased where Jesse's fingers had worried it. Mr. Hewell glanced at her and dialed the pager number on the card, and added the call back number. Then he hung up and focused on Jesse. "If you want to wait…."

The phone interrupted. Mr. Hewell glanced at it, raised his eyebrows, and picked it up. "Detective Lowrey, this is the Greenier Auction House in Moose River. There's a little gal here, name of…" he put his hand over the phone and squinted at Jesse.

"Jesse Marsh."

"Jesse Marsh. She said to call you about a saddle she found." Then he paused for a moment and said, "Miss Marsh is right here. It might be easier if I just let her explain everything to you." He handed the phone to Jesse and turned to the papers on his desk. Lauren and Jesse's grandfather waited in silence.

"Detective Lowrey?"

The police officer's deep voice filled the headset. "Yeah, Jesse. You found your saddle?"

"I found it on one of the auction tables."

"Did you check for your horse?"

Jesse bit her lip. She'd wanted to check for Starbuck. She glanced at Lauren. "No, we just came in here and reported to Mr. Hewell. Sorry."

Detective Lowrey chuckled. "No reason to be sorry, you did the right thing. Somebody could be watching the horse. The saddle too, for that matter, but with the saddle, taking it into the office can be explained easier than a big hubbub over a horse. Now, I have a plan. I want you to give the saddle back to…what was his name?"

"Mr. Hewell." The manager looked up from his

paperwork at the sound of his name.

"Right, Hewell. Give the saddle back to him and let them auction it off as if nothing happened. You buy it, make like you're bringing money into the office. Then, go home. I'll call the Moose River police and arrange a little rendezvous with our thief friend when he comes to pick up the money. I'll be right on my way."

"What about Starbuck?" The saddle didn't matter.

"Ask Mr. Hewell to have somebody check for him. If a horse meets his description, send your dad out to confirm it's him."

"My dad's not here, just Lauren and my grandpa."

"That's fine. Then I want you to let them auction your horse off, too. Don't you bid on him. Let your grandpa, like he's buying a gift for you. Got it?"

"Yes sir, I do." Jesse could barely breathe. Starbuck could be here. He might be hers again within a few hours.

"Good girl. Have you called your dad yet?"

"No, we called you first," Jesse said.

"Okay, I'll see if I can reach him, get him to come down with me. I think I have his work number here. You scared?"

"A little," Jesse admitted.

"Well, let me tell you, there will be police officers right there. Nothing will happen that they can't handle."

"Okay."

"Let me talk to Mr. Hewell again."

Jesse said goodbye and handed the phone back to Mr. Hewell.

"Hewell." The tall man listened for a while. He glanced at Jesse, and then at her grandfather. Then he hung up. "Tell me what your horse looks like."

"I have a picture of him." She pulled out her wallet.

"I should have known." Mr. Hewell smiled at her; wrinkles creased the corners of his eyes. Jesse's grandpa chuckled. The manager studied the photo for several minutes, and then tucked it in his shirt pocket. "I'll give it back to you after I check the pens. Wait here."

Jesse nodded and swallowed hard. She felt as if she was going to jump out of her skin. Please let Starbuck be there. Mr. Hewell picked up the saddle and headed out the door. Jesse pivoted in her chair to fill Lauren and her grandfather in on the plan to trap the thieves. Lauren grinned and her eyes sparkled. "Alright! Gonna bust some bad guys!" Jesse's grandfather nodded his head and said, "Let's hope Mr. Hewell finds Starbuck."

By the time Mr. Hewell returned, a short ten minutes later, Jesse's mouth had gone dry and she had to use the restroom. She stood. He shook his head. "I'm sorry. There's no palomino. I checked twice."

Jesse felt like the world had swallowed her whole. Of course the thieves wouldn't have brought him. It would have been too risky. She should have known that. But, she reminded herself, it wasn't over yet. She took a slow deep breath. Maybe when they caught the thieves, they'd learn something. Still, she had hoped Mr. Hewell would find Starbuck. Her grandpa put his hand on her elbow. "Come on, honey, let's go out and watch the auction, maybe get a hotdog and soda, too." He nodded to Mr. Hewell and guided her out. Lauren followed.

CHAPTER 8

Jesse squirmed and hoped she hadn't pick up a splinter. Could it be possible that the wood underneath her had hardened over the last hour? Mr. Hewell had long since sent a message to them informing them that the police had arrived and her saddle was coming up soon.

"You going to eat that?" Lauren asked. She reached for the cold hotdog that sat beside Jesse.

Jesse shook her head and wiped her forehead on the heel of her hand. She'd never seen a crowd that big at an auction before. They took up every available sitting space. She stretched her neck to get some fresh air. She looked over at her grandfather. His eyes never left the stage and between his feet sat the box with the hidden harness. He'd gotten the whole box for only seven dollars. For as long as she could remember she'd been coming to auctions with him. At first, her mom and dad came with them, but they'd always gotten bored quickly. Her parents had abandoned the two of them to enjoy the show together. Nowadays, she and her grandfather seldom had time to go to the auctions during her short visits. This should have been fun.

Jesse leaned close to Lauren. She whispered,

"You're my best friend, and I'm really sorry about earlier. When I wanted to go look for Starbuck, I mean. You were right."

Lauren, her cheeks stuffed, smiled at Jesse and shrugged. "It's okay, I'd have been the same way if it was Legs." Jesse smiled back. Lauren never let anything bother her. Why couldn't she be more like that? Why did everything feel so traumatic to her? Lately, she'd felt all weepy inside all the time. Especially now. She turned back to the auctioneer. If she concentrated on him, maybe the weepiness would go away.

The auctioneer carried on like a machine, one saddle after another, and his voice fell into a rhythm. His punctuated outbursts echoed off the metal walls, and added more drama to his chant. The crowd murmur swelled and fell away, like a tide, according to the pulse of the auctioneer's chant.

Jesse couldn't focus. What if someone tried to outbid her on the saddle? She'd have to keep bidding until it was hers again, no matter how high it went. What if the trap didn't work, and the thief remained free? They'd never find Starbuck. What if she missed the saddle, didn't see it auction? Somebody else would get it, the trap would be ruined, Starbuck would be gone and it would be all her fault. Her stomach churned.

Lauren nudged her, and Jesse snapped back to the stage to see her saddle held high. The auctioneer tapped the podium with his gavel and paused to make sure everyone centered on him. That wasn't the ordinary. Jesse supposed Mr. Hewell had asked him to do that, to let her know it was her time, and also to capture the thief's attention.

"Folks, here we have a nice English Stubben saddle. Looks to be a jumping saddle. It's a close contact, well broke in, well oiled, yet still fairly new. I'd guess it to be only around a year old. Yessiree folks, this one's a dandy. I see it going for a fair bit. Who'll give me $500, $500, $500. Lookin' for $500 dollars first bid, please."

He pivoted and swung his gavel, pointing it straight at Jesse. She knew that auctioneers often picked a person out of the crowd to personalize the sale, and draw the crowd's emotions into it. A good auctioneer would make people overbid because the emotional stakes were high. But, she also thought he did it to get her specific attention, in case she'd missed the first hidden warning from him. As if he didn't have all her attention anyway. The crowd took no notice and the volume of their voices had begun to swell again.

Jesse didn't know what to do. She'd never make a bid so pricey. But this saddle belonged to her, and she had to buy it. She moved her hand. Then she felt her grandfather's fingers on her arm as he whispered, "Not yet, honey. Don't appear to be too eager. We can't tip our hand." She gave a tiny nod. She'd wait and let someone else start the bidding.

"$500, $500, alright $300. Who'll give me $300 for this pretty saddle?" Nobody moved. Jesse felt the heat rise on her neck. $300? Her saddle? How could people not bid? Why didn't they open their eyes?

Lauren whispered, "Your saddle's one of the best Stubben makes. It's worth a lot more than $300."

"I know." Jesse frowned at the buyers sitting around the warehouse-sized room. Most people chatted with their neighbors and ignored the stage.

The auctioneer began again. He pounded the gavel and said, "This saddle is top of the line from Germany. That's right folks, made in Germany, where all the best jumping saddles are made. The manufacturer hand makes these babies. This saddle, brand new was probably around $1800. It's a pretty saddle, a well taken care of saddle. Now, who'll give $250 for it?"

For a moment, a hush fell on the crowd. Then a hand shot up over to the left. A barker spotted the bidder, a woman, and hollered at the auctioneer that he had a bidder. Jesse let out a sigh of relief. The auctioneer echoed the sigh and said, "That's better folks. I knew you could spot a bargain. I've got $250, who'll give me $300, $300? Who'll give me $300?"

Jesse raised her hand. A second barker pointed at her and called out a split second later. The crowd, as one, pivoted their heads her direction. Her whole body shook. She'd bid on things before at auctions. It reminded her of a game. The stakes had never been this high, though. Her grandpa squeezed her arm and whispered, "Here we go, honey."

Jesse smiled at her grandfather as another bidder shot up his hand at the price of $400. She wondered if the thief would bid against them just to bring up the price. She stood to try to see the bidder, but she couldn't pick him out. The chant moved on.

"$500, $500, how about you ma'am will you go $500?" He pointed at the first bidder and received a short nod. The barker on that side added his volume. The crowd relaxed, and a few conversations began again.

"Got $500, how about $600?"

Jesse shot up her hand again, and the barker on her side of the room chimed in his part.

"Thank you ma'am. $700, $700, $700. Anybody give $700?"

Lauren leaned over and whispered, "I've never been

to an auction before. This is kinda fun." Jesse smiled, but kept her eyes on the podium.

The auctioneer pointed toward where the gentleman sat, and again Jesse stood to try to see him. Nobody moved and after a moment, the barker turned and pointed at the first lady. He stabbed his finger at her again and again. She took awhile, but then she nodded. The barker sang, and then everyone on stage pointed at Jesse.

"Slowly." Her grandpa whispered.

Jesse would buy it at $750, of course, but she hesitated for a several moments. She sat down and frowned. She wanted to make it look like she couldn't decide. Silence closed on the crowd and all eyes flew to her face. None of the other saddles had brought near as much as this one. Jesse could see the tingle of excitement in the people that sat near her. Then she nodded once, like she was doing something she didn't really want to do.

The barker and the auctioneer spoke at the same time, drowning the first few words of the chant. "...hundred? $800?" The crowd's eyes dashed over to the rival bidder. No one spoke a word.

The woman didn't answer, and the auctioneer began to make it personal. "Ma'am, you'd look mighty fine in this saddle. It's made from the finest leather Europe has to offer. Just look at it. Come down here and feel it if you want. This saddle is worth more than a measly $800. I can't let it go for $750. I'll pull it off the block and offer it up again later. I remind you that new it was worth around $1800. It's been well taken care of since. And you can have it for the asking price of $800. Only $800. Will you give me $800?"

The bidder eased her chin into a slow nod, as if she were drugged. Still the crowd said nothing. Some of them in the back stood to watch.

The auctioneer turned to Jesse. "$850. Will you give $850 ma'am? Don't lose your chance at this wonderful saddle." Jesse didn't need to be talked into bidding again. She could see that the other lady was finished. She scanned the faces nearest her. Their eyes were glued to her. She thought some of the people were holding their breath. She gave a sharp nod.

"Thank you ma'am, I can see you know your saddles. $900, will you give $900?"

He pointed at the lady, but she shook her head, a grimace on her face. At $900, Jesse doubted that the saddle would be a bargain to anyone now. The auctioneer made the call general. "$900, $900? Will somebody give me $900?" Then he hesitated long enough to scan the room.

"Sold! $850 to Number..." The crowd collectively let out its breath and erupted into animated conversation.

Jesse held up her grandfather's bid number.

"Number 23." The auctioneer had to shout to make himself heard. "Next up, we have an Australian Stock Saddle, and let me tell you folks this one's a honey. It's got silver plates...."

Lauren whooped, and clenched Jesse's arm. Jesse smiled back, her jaw tense. It was over. The trap had been set, and now they had to wait to see if the thief would take the bait. Her grandfather grabbed his box of leather and they made their way back to the office. Mr. Hewell was waiting for them in the front office, standing in front of the two, now empty, desks. He held a steaming coffee cup in his hand. The aroma mingled with the buttered popcorn smell. It made Jesse's stomach tighten even more.

"Detective Lowrey called back to say he's picked up your dad and they're on their way down here. He told me to make sure you three didn't stick around, but went home. So, here's your receipt. The police will pick up your saddle and impound it for a little while. I guess they'll get hold of you later today, when they're done here."

Jesse hesitated a moment, then said, "We could wait in your office."

The manager shook his head, "No, I was told to physically escort you to your car if I had to. From what the Detective told me, these guys are real dangerous. Things could get nasty here. I even told my girls to get out." He swept his arm to indicate the two empty desks. "Now, do I have to chase you out, or will you go on your own?" He crossed his arms and stared down at them.

"Come on girls. They're treatin' us like kids, but I don't think we're gonna win this one. 'Sides, I know a few mules that are needin' some food this afternoon, yet. You can help me with that until that Detective and your Dad get there." Her grandpa tugged them toward the door.

CHAPTER 9

Once in the auction house parking lot, Lauren and Jesse's grandfather clambered into the truck. Jesse looked over her shoulder at the auction house door, just to check, and then joined them. As her grandfather started the truck and swung it in an arc, another pickup with an old blue stock trailer rattled into the parking lot, pulling a wave of dust behind it. Her grandfather stopped the truck and reached for the window handle. Lauren did the same. Above the clattering of the raising windows, Jesse's grandpa said, "Girls, I think we're just gonna sit here while this clears."

The dust cloud drifted around them and created waves and eddies like an ocean. It isolated the three of them in their own sphere separate from the rest of the world. Jesse's nose began to itch, and she fought the urge to rub it. Just before the sneeze came, she gave in and pinched her nostrils shut, stifling the sneeze. The dust began to dissipate in large patches and holes and Jesse caught glimpses of the square white steel rails of the paddocks. "Grandpa, Mr. Hewell told us to leave the sale barn, and we did. We're going home, like we said. But, the horses are right over

66

there. Could we drive by them on the way out? Check for Starbuck ourselves?"

Lauren leaned around her from the passenger's seat, winked at Jesse and added, "We don't even have to get out of the truck."

Her grandfather frowned, as but he didn't say 'No.'

"He might be there. Mr. Hewell might have missed him." Jesse paused.

Lauren said, "Please."

The dust cleared into a soft haze and her grandfather started the truck again. Jesse held her breath. He shifted the truck into gear and eased the vehicle over to the pens, crunching the gravel as they went. He rolled down his window and dust sifted onto his leg from the roof of the cab.

"Slowly, go slowly," Lauren whispered. She squeezed between Jesse, in the middle seat, and the dash to watch over the steering wheel. Jesse put her elbow on the back of the seat and crawled to her knees. Every pen held at least two horses, sometimes more. Chestnuts, Browns and Bays filled most of the pens. Some of the horses lowered their heads and shook dust out of their manes. Others sneezed globs of dust soaked slime from their noses. Jesse found that, though the pens had been cleaned recently, they still held the sharp reek of urine and manure from long overuse. Flies that dotted the necks and flanks of the beasts, sucking in blood and sweat, took occasion to buzz into the truck window.

A giant gray horse with a thick crested neck and wide muscular chest paced in the first pen. It raised its head to trumpet a challenge to the other horses. Then it pawed at the metal rails and a loud clanging note eclipsed all the other horse and truck sounds. The pen next to him stood empty. "Stud horse," said Jesse's grandfather and nodded his head.

"They won't get much for him."

As they passed the sixth paddock, a flash of blonde snapped Jesse's attention to it. That pen held four horses. Her heart jumped to her throat and she held her breath. It would be easy to miss Starbuck in a crowd like that. The horses grunted and shifted. Then, a honey-colored face swiveled toward Jesse. Instead of Starbuck's fine white-blonde mane, thick ropes of tangled black hair hung down over the horse's big-boned brow. A Buckskin. Not Starbuck. Jesse's heart plummeted back into her chest and crushed against her ribs. Not Starbuck.

When they finished the row, Jesse's grandfather turned the truck toward the exit and patted Jesse's leg. "Sorry, honey."

Lauren flopped back into her own seat by the window with a deep sigh. "Me, too," she said and gave Jesse a half smile.

"Thanks. At least we tried." Jesse smiled back. The words sounded hollow, even to her. She swallowed the lump in her throat and twisted in the seat to look out the back window. Again, the Buckskin lifted its head, as if watching her, mocking her. She felt cheated. The gray stud at the end whinnied and pawed at the rail again. She craned her neck to see the front door of the auction house. It could have been a still painting for all the movement she saw. Even Mr. Hewell's office window looked peaceful and empty. Now everything hinged on what happened inside there.

On the drive home, her grandfather chattered with Lauren about the lack of rain, the difference between mules and horses, and how to break an animal to harness. They tried to involve Jesse, but she only gave one-syllable answers. Jesse knew they thought they would preoccupy her mind, but it wasn't working. Thoughts of the Auction house and what might be happening there filled her head. Her mind's eye showed her a movie of the capture of the thieves and how they would divulge the location of Starbuck. She sighed and dropped her head back onto the top of the seat. She closed her eyes and tuned Lauren and her grandfather out.

"Jesse?" Lauren's voice.

Jesse didn't move. Maybe Lauren would think she was asleep.

"Jesse?" Lauren nudged her.

"What?" Jesse didn't lift her head from the seat back, but she opened her eyes.

"How do you know how high to go when you bid?"

"I don't know. You just do."

"But what if you pay too much for something?"

Jesse gritted her teeth and pretended she didn't hear. She concentrated on a big dent in the red roof of the cab. She felt like she could jump through her skin. She didn't want to be badgered or have to answer stupid questions from anybody. She wanted Starbuck back. Plain and simple. Everything else could go away.

After a moment, Lauren leaned into her and tried again. "Jesse? What if you pay too much for something?"

Jesse lifted her head and glanced over at her grandfather, hoping he'd answer the question for her, and then he and Lauren could carry on the conversation without her. He stared straight ahead at the road, quiet. She sighed again and turned her own attention forward. She wanted to scream for everyone to just leave her alone. She waited a moment, and then answered, making each word almost a separate sentence. "Only you can decide how much that thing is worth to you." Maybe Lauren would take the hint and stop talking.

"But how do you decide that?"

Jesse bit back a sarcastic remark and dropped her head onto the seat again, eyes closed, listening to the whine of the truck's fat old tires on the highway. It wasn't her friend's fault Starbuck had been stolen.

"Jesse?"

She refused to take her frustrations out on Lauren. No matter how tough things got. She replayed the movie in her head one more time.

"Jesse?"

Would they ever get back to the farm?

CHAPTER 10

When they reached the farm, Jesse's grandfather put Jesse and Lauren to work feeding the mules their special corn/bran mix that had been ordered for them from a local elevator. Then they fed the chickens and collected eggs. A broody hen puffed up her feathers and pecked at Lauren when she tried to slip her hand into the nest to take the eggs.

Every few minutes, Jesse poked her head around whatever corner she stood nearest and checked the drive. She kept her ears open for the outside phone bell, too. It slowed down their chores, but she couldn't help it. They should hear something soon. After chores, Jesse and Lauren went into the house to watch TV and wait.

Almost three hours later, a brown unmarked police car rolled up the gravel drive, its long antennas waving as it crunched to a standstill. Jesse and Lauren jumped down the porch steps to greet Jesse's father and Detective Lowrey.

"Well?"

"What'd you find out?"

"Did it work?"

"Did you catch them?"

Detective Lowrey nodded and held up his hands. "We caught one guy, alright. It was Mark Banks. He didn't suspect a thing. He just walked right in and demanded his money. You should have seen his face when we arrested him. We're holding him without bail."

Lauren's war holler swelled in the air. A covey of quail startled in the field across the road. They whirred off in panicked flight to find a safer hideaway. Someone clapped Jesse on the back, knocking her forward a couple steps. When she glanced over her shoulder, she saw her grandfather grinning behind her.

Jesse's dad frowned while Jesse rubbed her shoulder. He said, "He wouldn't say anything about his accomplice or Starbuck, though. From the papers at the auction house, we found an address near Rockwood, on Route 15, just south of town. We went there, but we didn't find anything. Just an empty white barn. And there weren't any horses around either."

Jesse felt stunned, like someone had slapped her across the face. They'd been so close. She was so sure they'd have a lead of some kind. She stood quiet and hugged herself. It must be just a bad dream. It had to be. She felt her lower lip begin to tremble and her eyes burned. She stared down at the ground, willing the tears to leave.

She felt as if she'd fallen into a deep well and someone had put the cover on it, locking her into her grief. It closed her in and surrounded her like those dark damp bricks around her grandpa's well. Starbuck. Her Starbuck. She'd been so sure they'd find him. Was there any way now? Any reason to hope? Or was he lost forever? Her heart heaved at that thought, and she shook it out of her head. She couldn't give up. It couldn't be over. Not yet.

The thought of that barn sprang into her mind. Rockwood was only 45 minutes away from the auction barn. It had to be more than just a fake address. It had to be.

Jesse waited until after her father and Detective Lowrey left and they'd eaten dinner. Then she piled on the flowered couch in the den beside Lauren. Lauren's favorite black and white Humphrey Bogart movie flickered on the TV in front of them. Lauren spoke Humphrey's lines with him. Jesse waited for a break in the dialogue and whispered, "I've been thinking about that barn."

Lauren leaned close and whispered back, "I know, me too."

"Those guys are smart."

Lauren nodded. "The police wouldn't know what to look for."

"I wish we could go there and check it ourselves."

"You don't think your Grandpa would take us?"

Jesse shook her head and frowned. "I don't know."

They watched Humphrey battle window shutters in a hurricane, and then Lauren leaned close over again and whispered, "Do you know how to drive?"

Jesse nodded and answered, "A little. Dad's been teaching me on the country roads."

"If we went slow, we'd be alright."

No one would stop them. She could tell her grandparents that she and Lauren wanted to go out for an evening walk to visit the mules. Sometimes that took some time, especially if they stumbled upon a loose calf. Her grandfather had parked the truck way down behind the barn when they'd hauled a few bales of hay to the mules. No one would hear it start. Still, the thought of lying to her family made her squirm inside. They trusted her. Would they understand how desperate she felt? Would they still trust her in the future? Of course, if she didn't tell them anything about where she was going, it technically wouldn't be a lie.

"This may be your only chance to find him."

Jesse stood and began to look for the truck keys in the house while Lauren went to check the truck. After a brief search in the den, Jesse headed into the kitchen. She found her grandmother there, mixing pungent spices with sweet crisp apples for pies. The heat from the oven only added to Jesse's unease. Her grandmother held out a wedge of seasoned apple for her. Guilt wormed through Jesse, making the apple taste bland. She glanced at the key rack. Empty. She hoped Lauren found the keys in the truck.

Jesse crossed the kitchen to the back porch to meet Lauren. Her grandfather looked up at her from a wicker rocker. He rustled the local newspaper he had open in front of him. The keys sat on the pine end table beside him. Now she had no choice but to lie.

She sat beside him. Why was this so hard? She could feel her heart pounding like hooves within her chest. "Nice night."

"Yep." He flipped to the next page.

"Grandpa, Lauren and I…." Her mouth dried and she stopped. Her stomach clenched into a rock hard knot. She could feel a flush begin to burn up her neck and onto her cheeks. She couldn't do it. She couldn't lie. It felt like a betrayal. And she didn't like that the lie made her feel sick and poisoned inside. She'd have to find a way to talk her grandfather into taking them. She started again, "Grandpa, Lauren and I want…."

He folded his newspaper in half and set it on the table beside the keys. He squinted at her. "You thinkin' you want to go look at that barn?"

Jesse felt her eyes widen and she stared at him. How did he know? She nodded and whispered, "Yes."

"Me, too. Your Dad'll skin me alive when he find's

out. But those men just aren't horsemen." Within two minutes they were on their way.

CHAPTER 11

On the edge of Rockwood, Jesse's grandpa pulled the truck into a Quick-Go gas station. A pimple-faced clerk slouched behind the cluttered counter, but straightened and smiled when he saw Lauren come in with Jesse. As he spoke, he focused on Lauren, even though Jesse's grandfather had asked the directions. The boy pointed toward the south. "This here's the old Toole Road. Go about five or six miles. You'll pass some grain elevators, and a couple a' brick two story houses with white columns. Big white columns. Then's your barn on the right. Can't miss it." Jesse turned around before she got into the truck and saw him at the door, watching Lauren leave. Boys always liked Lauren.

Toole Road ran straight through town. Then it curved and banked through the trees with sharp twisting turns for the next three miles. Jesse's grandfather's foot tapped the brakes in a continuous rhythm while the truck swerved back and forth like a drunken hero. Jesse and Lauren swayed against each other with each turn. Trees flipped past them, interspersed with hillside pastures that held staring midnight-black Angus cattle. A few pastures held horses of every color, except Palomino.

The sun hung an hour off the horizon, and tree shadows began to sharpen across the roadway when the road pulled straight again. Jesse and Lauren peered through the windshield, searching for the clerk's landmarks.

They passed a one-story brick home with columns. "Those columns aren't very big. Maybe the size of my waist, at the most," Lauren said.

"Our courthouse has bigger." Jesse turned to her friend.

"Half of our town has bigger."

"They were gray, too."

"Kinda makes you think you can't trust that guy, don't it?" Jesse's grandpa asked. "We're almost at mile seven, and I haven't seen any white barn yet."

Just then Jesse spotted a giant white barn sitting against the trees well back in a tiny clearing. It was on the left, instead of the right. Her grandfather grunted and said, "Wrong side of the road." He drove another mile, and then, when they found no other barn, turned around and pulled the truck onto the wheat field access road. They climbed out of the truck, gripping flashlights, and began to wind their way through the hip-high wheat back to the building.

As they got closer, Jesse's heart drummed harder and harder in her chest. This barn could hold the key to Starbuck's whereabouts. She studied the exterior of the barn for clues of some kind. Someone had loved this barn once, but it had been a long time ago. Paint chips had flaked off the siding and the green trim, showing bare weathered wood beneath. Hail pox marks made the shingles look black with tiny green dots instead of the solid green they must have been. The once green doors sagged to the ground, half-fallen off their hinges. Memories of her tack room door jumped out at her and she felt herself begin to shake.

She swallowed hard and hugged herself while her grandpa shifted one of the doors and peeked inside. He motioned them to wait and wedged his head and thick chest through the opening into the dark interior, easing all the way inside with a flashlight. Jesse glanced around at the dark trees. It would be so easy for someone to hide there. Lauren flashed her a nervous smile. She must have been thinking the same thing, too. Then, Jesse's grandfather's face appeared at the door and he nodded. Jesse took a deep breath of relief and realized she'd held her breath the whole time he was inside. She smiled at him as she and Lauren climbed into the dark interior.

Dusky light filtered through a far corner of the barn roof where a heavy tree branch poked through. Jesse flicked her flashlight beam that way and saw rain rotted straw piled beneath it on a partial loft that encircled the barn. She let her beam follow the straw that had escaped the bonds of twine before it rotted and saw it had tumbled into one long sliding pile. Dark piles of raccoon droppings and corncobs dotted the cascade. She traced the edge of the loft and saw an old collar some proud plow horse had worn years before. Rips crisscrossed its old leather and dust caked it at least an inch thick. Lauren's and Jesse's grandfather's flashlight beams flicked over the interior, also. Shadow ghosts shivered alive in the corners, but other than that the barn looked bare.

Jesse heaved her chest in a sigh. If Starbuck, or any horse, had been there, the place would still smell like him, even a little. Not like it did now: old, dry, dusty, and beneath the rotted corner, moldy. Beside her, Lauren sneezed and then glanced at her. "It looks pretty empty"

"Yeah." Jesse felt the hope her heart held begin to wither up. Her throat tightened and she looked away from Lauren and her grandfather.

As if he knew her thoughts, Jesse's grandfather added, "Don't give up. There might be somethin' small here. Somethin' that might lead us further." He scuffed the barn floor, and started sifting through the dried mulch. Dust billowed upwards in a ball shaped cloud.

"I'll check the loft," Lauren said. She crossed to the ladder and began a slow climb.

"Be careful of holes and rotten boards, young lady," Jesse's grandfather called after her.

Jesse suppressed her own urge to sneeze and began to look around. Cobwebs strung across the rafters and stretched from posts to the floor in thick woven patterns. A large yellow and black spider lurked in the middle of one. He looked like he'd been undisturbed for a long time. That meant the police hadn't done a good job searching.

There might still be something. Any chance was worth it. For almost an hour they scoured the barn for clues. Lauren even spooked a raccoon out of the loft and it crawled, scolding, out through the roof. Nothing else turned up.

As they drove back through the town of Rockwood in the dusk, none of them said anything. Jesse stared out the open passenger window beside her. The wind held a soft fragrance of blooming lilacs. Little kids chased fireflies with mason jars. Some boys played basketball in a driveway, their ball thump-thumping on the concrete. Couples sat illuminated by porch lights and citronella candles, serenaded by singing crickets. These people all had normal happy lives. Why couldn't she? That barn had been her last hope, and they'd found nothing.

She'd tried being positive, but it had gotten her nowhere. She'd done everything she knew how to do, but it hadn't been enough. All her work had only raised her hopes so they could plummet deeper. So what if she had her saddle, it didn't do her much good without a horse. And she didn't want any other horse. If she couldn't have Starbuck, then she wouldn't have any horse. Tears cut their way from her heart into her eyes and she turned her head further to the side, letting them fall.

On the edge of Rockwood, near the Quick-Go, Jesse saw a long low barn that stretched across a hilltop. Lights from open upper stall doors pierced through the twilight, and a large group of horses grazed near the fence by the road. Jesse remembered that barn from the first half of the trip. The horses hadn't been let out then. She barely made out a dark horse that raised his head and watched the truck as they passed. Just like Starbuck would have. He'd known the sound of every vehicle her family owned. The horse wheeled and charged beside them, making playful kicks her direction. Starbuck would have done that, too. She'd never stop hurting this time, she knew it. And she'd never have another horse.

The horse reached the end of the pasture and bounced stiff-legged to a stop, and then lifted his nose and whinnied.

"Stop! Stop the truck!" Jesse screamed. Panic pierced her and made her dizzy. A sharp sweet taste flooded her mouth. That was Starbuck's whinny! She knew it from any other horse. It had a peculiar uplift note at the end, like he questioned everything around him. She'd always been able to pick it out from a group.

"What the...?" Jesse's grandfather almost stood up on the brakes as he skidded the truck to a halt and piloted it onto the gravel roadside.

"What is it?" Lauren's voice rang close in Jesse's ear, her weight leaning over Jesse's shoulder.

Jesse at last found the handle and she wrenched the door open. They both tumbled onto the ground.

Jesse scrambled to her feet and bolted back toward the horse, brushing her hands across her jeans. The gravel dislodged from her skin, stinging. She whistled Starbuck's private call that she'd taught him meant treats. The horse whinnied in reply and paced along the corner of the fence until she got there. When she reached him, she drew a shaking hand across the fence and traced the contours of the dark horse's face. She knew this face. Fine, soft bangs floated down over the horse's brow. She knew this hair, too. So what if it wasn't blonde? The horse nickered against her shoulder and nuzzled her hair.

Lauren came up behind her. "What I can see sure looks like him."

"It IS him. I know it." Jesse climbed over the pasture fence, crowded by the horse. Lauren joined her a split-second later.

"They dyed him black!"

"I can't see," Jesse said almost to herself, frowning. Her heart threatened to hammer right through her ribs and she thought she might throw up, her belly hurt so bad. The horse followed her every step, nuzzling for the promised treats. He crowded against her, bumping her and she staggered to the side a few steps. She said to Lauren, "Hold him still so I can see."

Lauren captured the black's head, and the horse snuffled at her hair. Jesse turned to go back to the truck for a flashlight, but her grandpa met her at the fence with one. As he handed it to her, he said, "Hurry Jess, I don't want to get caught trespassin'. And if that is him, it means that other thief's here someplace."

She took the flashlight from him and put her fingers over the lens. Then she turned the beam into a narrow band. Returning to the horse, she leaned down, and began to search the horse's belly and legs. The horse didn't make it easy, he tried to turn and twist every direction she moved. She placed her hand on his warm side, and continued her search. The thieves had to have missed something. Somewhere…. Then she saw it. Standing, she pointed the flashlight to a small tuft of palomino hairs almost hidden in the wrinkles behind one of the horse's front legs. "There!"

Lauren patted her pockets, found her cellphone, and pressed it into Jesse's hand. "Call."

"And hurry up about it. I don't fancy gettin' caught out here by anyone," Jesse's grandpa added, voice low. Jesse clicked off the flashlight and peered into the dark. He continued, "There's still one thief on the loose. He could be here. In that barn up there, maybe."

"We could wait in the truck." Lauren's voice sounded tiny, like she'd swallowed it.

"I won't leave Starbuck," Jesse hissed. She fumbled with her wallet. She'd put Detective Lowrey's card in there somewhere. She found it after what seemed eons, and, after she put her wallet back into her hip pocket, she coded Detective Lowrey's pager into the phone. Then she hung up to wait. The night began to crispen to a cooler temperature, and Jesse could almost hear the dew as it settled to the ground.

Lauren's phone chirruped and Jesse stabbed at the neon yellow answer button. Instead of the detective's voice, her father's filled her ear. "Jesse?"

She bit her fingernails into her palm. How she

wanted to scream the words. "We found him."

"Where?" After she told him, he asked, "Are you there with him?"

"Yes," she breathed.

"Listen to me. We're headed back your way. Get away from there. Go down the road a bit, and wait for the police. I'll call them now. Do you hear me?"

"Dad, I-"

"Don't argue. Do it." Then he hung up.

Jesse closed the phone and handed it back to Lauren. She turned to Starbuck and said more to him than anyone else, "We need to go wait down the road." She traced her finger down his cheekbone. It felt like she would die to leave him. She wrapped her arms around his neck, and squeezed his neck tight. Her eyes blurred when she turned around and jogged to join Lauren and her grandfather at the truck. She knew her dad was right. Of course. He was always right. And he'd used that 'do NOT disobey' tone with her. It was just so hard to leave, now that she'd found Starbuck again. But, that thief could be watching them right now. The darkness held her just as captive as her horse.

A soft breeze gusted past Jesse. The bush, on the fence line to her right, shook. Was it just the breeze? She slowed her jog to a walk. The moon disappeared behind a monumental cloud. For a moment, she forgot to breathe and she squinted into the inky night. She stopped and checked in every direction. Nothing moved. The corner of the pasture faced her on the left, maybe seven feet away. She began to inch her way over to it, tiny step by tiny step. She never took her eyes off the bush. A shape that shaded denser than the black night disengaged from the bush's shadow with a twig snap. A shot of energy bolted through Jesse, and she rose up off her heels to begin her flight. Then the shadow mooed. A cow. A dumb, stupid cow on the other side of the fence. Jesse hung her head, and smiled. Relief folded down her body and her knees wobbled like a jellyfish. She turned toward the fence and the road.

Jesse kept watch all around her while she climbed the fence and headed for the truck. As she climbed in beside Lauren, she glanced back toward the barn. A shadow crossed one of the lights, blocking it. The row of lights looked like a Jack-o-lantern smile with a tooth missing. "Look," she whispered and pointed.

Lauren leaned forward. "I don't see anything." The lights sparkled through all the windows again and gave no hint of any presence.

"Someone was just there. I saw him move." Jesse blinked her eyes. Someone had been there, at least she though so. "We need to park the truck down the road, in case someone's watching us." Lauren's face paled, and Jesse's grandpa set his lips into a thin line as he started the truck and eased it out onto the road.

CHAPTER 12

"Well," said Detective Lowrey, "that's enough evidence to impound the horse. We'll need to verify him against any photos or vet records you have, though." Detective Lowrey straightened from the horse's side and walked over to the fence. He crossed in front of the beam from his headlights and, for a moment, Starbuck and the other five horses vanished. Then the detective stepped out of the light and all six horses reappeared.

"We had a Coggins test done on him for the show season, but I don't have it with me," Jesse offered. She glanced at the sky. The cloud that had blocked the moon earlier hadn't left, and other clouds piled against it. A chill draft darted down from them. She turned up the collar on her father's denim jacket, pulling it tighter against her. Lightning hadn't sparked through the sky yet, but it wouldn't be long.

The detective raised his eyebrows and twisted his head toward Jesse's father. "Coggins test?"

"It's a test to check for a fatal disease, Equine Infectious Anemia. The show circuits require proof the horse is clean. I could call the Sauciers next door, have

85

them find our copy of the Coggins test and fax it to your office. We could get a local vet to come out and check it."

"And that has a photo of your horse on it?"

"Better. It has markings and hair patterns." Jesse's father paused and ran his fingers through his hair. He added, "We're not leaving here without this horse." Then he crossed his arms and leaned back against the fence.

Jesse stepped next to him and hooked her hand into the crook of his elbow. She stared at Detective Lowrey. Lauren left the nearby group of haltered horses and came to stand next to Jesse.

Jesse's grandpa spoke softly from across the fence, "We can impound him at my place. That'll keep him safe until we get the vet's okay."

The Detective flicked his eyes from face to face, but stopped and held Jesse's gaze. Then he nodded slowly and said, "Okay. Call who you need to. Get that test faxed to my office as soon as possible." Then he scraped across the fence to the other side again while Jesse's dad pivoted away with his cellphone and stepped into the dark. Detective Lowrey paused and asked Jesse's grandfather, "You got enough room for the rest of these horses? I got a feeling more of these horses may be stolen, too. The state will pay you for any expenses you have until I can check on them."

Her grandfather's voice took on a thoughtful note. "Well, I suppose I could move those mules of mine over with the cattle for a few days, and there's that abandoned house behind ours that could be renovated to hold a few stalls...."

Detective Lowrey nodded again. "That'll work." Then he said to Jesse, "We didn't find anyone up at the barn. The owners of the property said they rented it to a man that fits the description of Mark Banks. He would let the horses out at night. He worried a lot about sunbleach on the horse's coats, and kept them blanketed and stalled during the day. That's how he hid the paint."

The lights of a passing car danced across the group, adding false shadows that Jesse thought looked like ghosts. Her dad swung back to them. "The Sauciers said they could get the Coggins to you tonight, yet. They have a fax machine in their office."

"I'll call my vet to pick it up at the local police station and meet us at home." Jesse's grandpa reached for the phone from her dad. "Then I'll just run home and fetch up my trailer." He jerked his head in a short decisive nod, and then he focused on the phone in his hand. After half a moment, he said, "Jess, maybe you better dial this for me."

It only took a moment to arrange for the veterinarian to meet them with the Coggins, but it took nearly an hour for Jesse's grandfather to drive home and return with the truck. Soon, however, Starbuck and the other five horses were on the way to Jesse's grandpa's farm. Lauren decided to ride ahead in the truck with Jesse's grandpa. Jesse and her father rode in the detective's car behind. Jesse hoped they'd get home before the storm broke. Lightening flashed sparks that reflected from the road, and the air smelled thick, like rain.

Detective Lowrey shook his head at Jesse in the rearview mirror. "I just don't see how you could have known it was your horse."

Jesse shrugged, "I just knew."

Her dad laughed. "There's nothing that can separate this girl from her horse. Every spare moment of the day she and Lauren are out there working, brushing and playing with their horses."

"My wife and I never had a daughter. We tried, but

ended up with four boys. I guess boys aren't like that." The detective chuckled. Almost twenty minutes later, they pulled into the farm drive. A long blue station wagon waited there, beneath the canopy of trees. Jesse's grandma and a square older man with glasses came out of the house to meet them.

The man identified himself as Dr. Caine. When all the horses had been unloaded, he asked Jesse, "Now, which is the wonder horse? I've heard so much about him from your Grandma and Grandpa these past few years I feel honored to finally meet him."

Jesse laughed and patted her horse's shoulder. "This is Starbuck."

Her horse bobbed his head and sidestepped to stare at the big-boned, chestnut gelding that Lauren led past. It had gotten out of the trailer shaky and white with lather. Now, as she let the gelding loose in the pasture, it kicked up its heels and wheeled around to play night tag with the other horses. The mules paced the nearby fence beside curious cows.

"Well, let's get Starbuck in the light and get this done before the storm breaks. Though," Dr. Caine tilted his face toward the single patch dark sky that showed through the trees, "it doesn't look as bad as it did half an hour ago. Maybe it'll miss us after all."

Jesse looked up at the patch of sky also. The clouds had opened up a little, and a star peeked through. She turned back to watch Dr. Caine.

He shrugged and inspected the faxed Coggins test in his hands. "According to this test, though, this horse is a palomino. I see why you need the Coggins test to identify him." He glared over his glasses at the horse. He walked around the horse, and twice stepped forward to inspect an area. As he made his way back to the horse's head, he said, "Well, I can't say for certain, but as certain as these things are, this is certainly her horse." He chuckled at Jesse.

Jesse let out her breath and smiled back. She knew this was Starbuck, but she'd been afraid they might not be able to prove it. Lauren grinned at her and held up her crossed fingers.

Detective Lowrey tapped his finger on the top rail of the fence and said, "Right. I'll get on the machine tomorrow and see if these other horses match up with any theft reports."

"Can we shave him?" Lauren squinted her eyes at the detective.

"You don't like him black?" Dr. Caine chuckled as he packed his case. "I'll be back tomorrow afternoon to check the others. I'm in trouble enough with my wife as it is, running out on her bridge game like this."

Detective Lowrey nodded slowly. "Yeah, go ahead and shave him. Let me get some pictures of him like this though. Is he scared of the flash?"

Jesse shook her head. "No, I've taken pictures of him ever since we got him. He's used to them by now."

Detective Lowrey smiled in the light of the lamp and said to her father, "Another difference between girls and boys." The detective fetched his camera from his car and took a photo. Starbuck perked his ears and arched his neck at the flash. After he took a photo from each side of Starbuck and the front and back, Detective Lowrey said, "Well, that does it. I think I'll head back up north."

"I may know the owner of the Bay Gelding." Jesse told them about the flier.

He nodded and then faced Jesse's father. "You need a ride home?"

"What do you say, Jess?" Her dad's dark eyes met hers.

"Go ahead." Jesse's grandma said, "All they're goin' to do is spend all their time with that horse." She smiled at the girls.

Still, he hesitated a moment longer, then smiled and said, "Alright. Jess, honey, I'll be here first thing tomorrow morning."

"It's almost tomorrow morning now," grumbled Jesse's grandfather.

Jessie tried to smile. She felt kinda weepy. Not the sad kind, but the happy I'm-so-glad-it's-over kind. She wished he could stay, but she knew she was being silly. "I'll be fine, see you in the morning." She hugged him as much as she could with Starbuck bumping and snuffling her.

Later that night, her Dad called just as she began to fall asleep. "Hey. How are you doing?"

"I'm so glad we found him!" she replied.

"Me too, honey. Me too!"

CHAPTER 13

That night, every time Jesse let herself drift off into sleep, she dreamed of stolen horses and shadows that came out of the darkness at her. Several times, she woke herself with a start, rose and checked out the window for Starbuck. The sky tinged with a bright rose streaked dawn when she decided to get up. She sat on the porch, wrapped in a blanket. Her nose ran and her breath almost steamed as it left her mouth. Birds sang their morning processional, and Starbuck grazed in the pasture nose-to-nose with one of the rescued horses.

Her grandfather joined her half an hour later with two cups of coffee. They sat in silence until he'd finished his cup, then he went to do his chores. "Looks like you've had a tough night, missy. Just sit there, and let me take care of the beasts." By the time he'd finished, Jesse's father had arrived along with a phone call from a local newspaper.

"Miss Marsh? My name is Haley Willette. I'm with The Jackman Herald. I'd like to do a story about you and your horse. I'll interview you about his theft, and then later, your recovery of him. Maybe I'll take some photos, too." She paused a moment, and then added, "May I come by and speak to you today?"

Jesse considered. A story in the newspaper would make her into some kind of hero. She didn't want that. Then again, it might help alert people to the dangers of horse theft. Most people thought horse theft, or 'rustling', was just a history lesson. "Today's fine. Do you know how to get here?"

"Yes, I do. See you about 10."

Jesse clicked the phone off and dropped it onto its cradle. Speaking of horse rustling, her grandfather had given her an idea last night. She didn't want to say anything about it yet; she didn't want to jinx it. Besides, she had some thinking to do.

Lauren came out of the kitchen chewing on a donut while Jesse told her father about the interview. Dust powdered out of her friend's mouth. "We're going to be in the news?" She shoved the rest of the donut into her mouth and began to lick her fingers.

Jesse nodded. "Yeah, at least Starbuck will be."

"Fantabulous."

Jesse's father chuckled. "I think it's a good idea, you might find the owners of some of the other horses."

Jesse could see Starbuck through the window as he grazed in the pasture. In the bright light of morning he looked to be a dingy black, blotched with patches of almost dark brown where the dye didn't take as well. She grimaced at Lauren and stood up.

"Where are you going?" her dad asked. A grin deepened the creases around his eyes.

Her grandpa snorted. "As if you didn't know. They've already brushed him once this morning. Came in just before you got here."

Jesse's grandmother shook her finger. "You two

leave the girls alone. Jesse, you go right on outside and be with your horse."

Jesse and Lauren raced for the pasture. They detoured past the shed just long enough to pick up a pair of clippers.

By Ten O'clock, Jesse, Lauren, and Starbuck were surrounded by piles of blackish fluff. Puffs of the hair skidded across the pasture and hooked on branches of the trees. Jesse's father leaned on the fence watching the progress. A green and brown Bronco pulled into the driveway and a lean athletic woman with honey colored hair exited. She carried a notebook with her. "Hi. I'm Haley Willette," she said, as she got close. She reached to shake Jesse's father's hand.

"Ray Marsh." He shook her hand. "This is Jesse and Lauren." He pointed to each of them in turn.

"And this is Starbuck I see here?" Haley slid between the rails of the fence and ran her fingers along his neck, speaking quiet words toward Starbuck's ear.

Jesse glanced at Lauren. They didn't like people who didn't like horses. This woman had shown herself worthy of friendship. Lauren raised her eyebrows. Jesse's dad grinned at them and winked.

As if Haley read Jesse's mind, she said, "We used to have horses when I was young. I even took lessons from a boarding stable when I moved away to college, just to keep legged-up. I always planned to buy myself a horse as soon as my career settled. Time just got away from me I guess." She grimaced.

"How did you find out about Starbuck?" Jesse's dad asked.

Haley chuckled, "You guys are big news around here. The whole town's talking about you. Also, my ex-husband is a police officer. He helped with the arrest at the auction house. He also heard the call go out on the scanner last night." She paused and then frowned. "I see you've shaved Starbuck. I would have liked to have gotten a 'before' picture, but I suppose the police have one?" She glanced at Jesse's dad.

He nodded.

"Alright. Why don't we start with the story itself, then progress into these other animals..." her gesture included the mules, which grazed near the adjoining fence. As if understanding Haley's words, Nattie pinned her ears back and whirled away. Lauren giggled as Haley continued. "...Then we can end up with you giving some tips about how to prevent thefts, or at least make it easier to recover stolen horses and tack. I want a few photos with you, Jesse, and your dad; definitely you and Starbuck anyway."

Haley listened as Jesse told the story. She only interrupted to ask the occasional question about Jesse's feelings at different points in the story. When Jesse finished, Haley didn't speak for a moment, but then she turned to Jesse's father and began to ask questions. Jesse noticed that Haley's voice cracked as she spoke.

"Okay," she said at last, scratching Starbuck on the hip as she walked past, "Let's talk about these horses." She frowned at the nearby mules. "I didn't realize there were any mules involved. My ex-husband didn't tell me."

Jesse smiled as Nattie again flattened her ears. "They're my grandpa's. They belong here."

"Oh. But the rest of these were with your horse, right?"

Jesse nodded as they strolled over to the group of refugee horses. The animals rolled their eyes at the humans, but they stayed put. Jesse's father and Lauren trailed behind with Starbuck.

"How many of these horses do you think were dyed?"

Jesse answered, "Most of them are the colors you see. The thieves were smart. They just changed subtle points. Like that bay you see; he's had a star painted over."

"How can you tell?"

Jesse's dad answered as he caught the horse, "Pink skin." The other horses clustered around, jealous for attention.

Haley said, "Yeah, now I remember. If they're born white, the skin is pink." She inspected the bay's head while Jesse's father held him near. Then she stepped away and tapped her own head, "See, its still there somewhere. It's just dusty."

"That chestnut has four white socks," Lauren pointed to the square stock horse she'd held the night before. Like the other horses, his bones stuck out in points and his ribs made solid stripes along his sides. All four legs had been painted an orange-brown in an effort to match his coat color. "The thieves kept blankets or hoods and boots on the horses during the day, so no one would see the paint."

"It should be easy to find this guy's owners. Actually, all these horses were quite beautiful in their normal appearance and their prime condition." Jesse's father shook his head. Jesse saw the anger that stretched across his face. "They're going to take a long time to recover. Even Starbuck, who was new to the group and not as badly damaged yet, has some healing to do."

"I understand the police only caught one of the thieves, and that the other one is still at large. How does that make you feel, Jesse?" Haley asked, facing to her.

Jesse bit her lip. It just plain scared her. She knew

she needed to answer, but her she didn't quite trust her voice.

Her dad put his arm around her and answered for her. "I think we're all a little anxious that he be caught, but until he is, the best we can do is let people know he's still out there and how they can best protect themselves against him and others like him."

None of them of them spoke for a long time. Jesse watched as Haley focused on one animal and then another. Pain filled her eyes. The horses, bored with the humans, had wandered to snatch at different patches of grass. Shadows from jutting bones chased across the horse's hides. Eventually Haley cleared her throat and asked, "What will you do if you don't find the owners?" She looked first at Jesse's father, but then she shifted her gaze to Jesse.

"We think we know the owner of the Bay gelding over there, but I don't know if the police have been able to reach him yet." Jesse glanced at her father. She had wanted think about her idea some more before she spoke to her dad. But the timing might be better now. "I have an idea for the rest. Well, it's Grandpa's idea really. It needs some work and it may not work at all. There are whole farms established to care for abused and neglected horses. Grandpa said we could renovate that old house behind here and put in some stalls for these horses."

Lauren chimed in, her eyes shining. "If we can't find the rightful owners, we could foster them out, or even let families adopt them."

Jesse held her breath and waited.

Her father didn't even pause before he answered, "I think that's a great idea, Jess. We could screen the adopting families to ensure the horses would be well looked after. We could also have visitation rights to check on them. I do see a few problems, but we can try it. That is, if we can convince your grandpa to be a temporary way station for awhile."

"Convince Grandpa what?" Startled the small group turned around to find the old man standing behind them with his hands on his hips.

Jesse quickly outlined her idea to him. She added her best 'please Grandpa' look at the end.

Her grandpa stared off into the distance while he listened. When Jessie finished speaking, he said slowly, "Well..., I got no problems with it." He raised his voice to be heard above Lauren's and Jesse's whoops. A couple of the horses wheeled and shied away. At the fence, the mules flicked their ears, but mostly ignored them. "IF it don't cost me nothin' and the state pays me for feed like they said," he finished.

Haley said, "You probably could get several organizations and businesses to contribute money and materials for the barn renovation and feed. No doubt a few veterinarians would contribute their services if needed. I could work it into the story and people could get in touch with you to volunteer their support."

They began making plans, and Haley threw in occasional comments and suggestions. Jesse listened with only half a mind. Haley had put a voice to the small fear inside her. She could feel it push at her lungs and twist in her gut. That second thief was still out there, somewhere, and neither she nor Starbuck would be safe until he was caught.

CHAPTER 14

Haley left at noon, her bronco kicking up dust as it skidded down the rocky driveway. Jesse and Lauren went into the house for a quick lunch, and then returned to the pasture. Starbuck had sidled up next to a tall chestnut mare, the thinnest of the group. The spaces between her bones showed as deep ruts on her dull coat, and her ribs resounded with a thud when her burr matted tail beat against it.

Lauren sputtered her lips. "That mare's gonna take some work."

Jesse nodded. "I thought we'd bang her tail. Cut it off maybe three or four inches below the end of her tail bone."

"We should roach her mane too. It'd take hours and at least a gallon of baby oil to untangle that mess." As if on cue, the mare shook her head, and the solid band of burred mane flopped from side to side.

"Definitely roached." Jesse grimaced and reached for the clippers.

Lauren grabbed the halter and headed across the pasture to the mare as Jesse's dad wandered out onto the porch. He stretched, reaching toward the sky, and then jogged down the stairs toward the pasture. "I'll give you a

98

hand.”

By the time Dr. Caine drove up the drive, almost an hour later, they were still working on the mare. The old vet chuckled when he climbed out of his car. “Looks like you three have been workin’ hard.” He reached back into the wagon for his bag, shut the door, and joined them in the pasture. He motioned toward the mare. “We might as well start with her.”

Pulling out his stethoscope, he listened to her lungs, and then moved to her stomach to hear the gut noises. After spending quite a few minutes there, he straightened. “Girls, I believe this mare is pregnant.”

Jesse frowned. “Pregnant? Will she be alright?”

“What about the baby?” Lauren asked.

“Well, the longer she waits to have it, the stronger and healthier she and the baby will be. I’m gonna give you a recipe for a high-vitamin tonic to mix in her feed.”

“When do you think she’s due?” Jesse’s dad asked.

“Hard tellin’, the shape she’s in.” He stepped back and stared at her tummy. “I’d say no closer than a couple months. I’ll draw some blood and see if we can get the lab to give us a better guess on her due date.”

He drew the mare’s blood and gave her vaccinations and a shot of penicillin. “Just for good measure. He opened her mouth to find her age. “Her teeth aren’t all capped yet, though four of them are filled in. I think she must be somewhere between two and three. She’s too young to be in foal and in this bad of shape. We’ll be lucky if we don’t lose both her as well as the foal.”

Lauren poked her finger toward the mare’s upper lip. “What’s that?”

Dr. Caine pulled up her lip. Dark blue dots formed lines on the pink flesh. “Looks to be a tattoo. Got a registered horse here, girls." He let go of the mare's lip and walked around to view her from the side again. The mare waggled her lip back and forth as she twisted her neck to watched him. "I think she's a thoroughbred. You might be able to find her owners through the Jockey Club."

"Next horse." He waved Lauren and the mare away while Jesse brought the bay gelding. When he had gone through all five of the horses and Starbuck, he again stared at the mare for several minutes. Then he collected his equipment and headed to his station wagon. Just before he left, he said, "I'll be back in a few days to check on that mare again. She worries me."

As she watched the Dr. Caine's car rattle down the drive, Lauren came up behind her. "The mare needs a name."

"She already has a name. A registered name. As soon as we find her owners, they'll want her back. There's no point in naming her for just a few days." Jesse trudged toward the house, suddenly tired.

"You can do what you want, but I'm gonna call her Kula." Lauren nodded beside her.

Jesse's father frowned, glancing from her to Jesse and back again. His eyebrows furrowed in a deep 'V' on his forehead. He opened his mouth to speak, but Lauren cut him off.

"It's from the Trobriand Islands off the coasts of New Guinea and Australia. It means 'sacred gift-giving process'."

They reached the porch, and Jesse started to tug herself up the steps with the handrail. What she needed was a nap. Hearing tires crunch on the driveway, she stopped. A gray pickup pulled up the drive and three men climbed out of the cab. Four more jumped out of the bed. One was an older man, and another was a boy of about 15.

Jesse's grandfather came out of the house. And the older man of the group reached out to shake his hand. "I'm Haley's dad, and these are her brothers. She called us and told us about your needin' help with those stolen horses you found. She said you're renovatin' a barn. A couple of us are carpenters, and we're all handy with a hammer. We can donate time if you have the materials. We have tools, just show us where to start."

CHAPTER 15

Three days later, on Saturday, Jesse led Starbuck up the ramp into the trailer for the trip home. The sun shone bright, with not a cloud in the sky. A gentle breeze sifted through the grass and trees and any remnant puddles had long since dried. It seemed as if the rainy spell had ended. If she'd been at home, she thought she'd have gone for a trail ride. As it was, Jesse thought she'd never seen a better day for the drive. Starbuck pranced up the ramp beside her and pawed at the floor of the trailer.

She shook her head, laughing. Over her shoulder, she said to Lauren, "Do you see how frisky he is? Somehow I think he should at least be as tired as I am." She fastened Starbuck's halter to the breakaway tie strap in the trailer and patted his neck.

"Yeah, how many calls did we get?"

Jesse shrugged as she rejoined Lauren outside. "I don't know, but we raised almost a thousand dollars to take care of the horses."

"A thousand! I didn't think it was that much. I thought most of it was feed and hay. Wow." Lauren knit her eyebrows together. "We really could make this a rescue farm."

Jesse nodded. Together, she and Lauren lifted the loading ramp and locked the trailer. Jesse's dad emerged from the house with her and Lauren's matched suitcases down the stairs and to the truck. He stowed the suitcases into the back beside his brown sports bag and slammed the tailgate shut. Facing Jesse, he said, "I think that's it. Better go tell your grandparents goodbye."

Jesse's grandmother met them on the porch. "Your grandpa just went out to the barn to turn the mules out. He'll be right back." She wiped her aged hands on her apron, and then untied it, laying it over the arm of one of the wicker rockers. When she turned to hug her, Jesse could see that her eyes sparkled with tears. "We sure miss you when you're gone, Jesse."

"I miss you, too." Jesse held onto her grandmother as tight as she could. She felt as if leaving them was leaving her security behind.

Her grandfather's heavy boots clunked up the steps. He said, "We'll see you at the Classic."

Jesse pulled back from her grandmother. She shook her head at him. "No, I'm not ready. I just got Starbuck back and we'd need too much time to practice."

"I think it might be a good idea for you to go, Jess. There's plenty of time for you to pull Starbuck together enough to place somewhere in the ribbons."

Jesse shook her head and replied, "No, I don't think so, too much has happened. It'd take forever." She jutted her jaw out, hating the tiny shake that crept her voice. She reached to hug her grandpa good bye.

"No it wouldn't, not if we worked together." Lauren said from behind her.

Jesse's grandfather whispered in her ear, "Goodbye, honey. Now don't you worry about that mare none. We'll keep an eye on her. If you decide to go to the show, we'll come watch you."

Jesse let go of him and smiled. They never missed any of her shows, no matter how small the competition. "I really don't think I'll go."

She hated to leave them so soon, but she was anxious to get Starbuck home. Once one the road, she stared out the windshield at the yellow lines that flipped past on the center of the highway. Further ahead, the road glared with the white hot of the summer sun. She wanted to sink into the ripples from the heat of that sun and hide forever. When would she stop being scared?

After about an hour on Highway 95, they pulled into a little gas station. Jesse's father pumped the gas into the truck, and then went inside to pay. Jesse and Lauren scurried to the bathroom.

When the two of them came out, an old green Plymouth pulled alongside the trailer and eased past. The paint had faded and the wax had bleached to a dull cream over-color. Scrapes and scratches criss-crossed around the doors and fenders. The black convertible top had holes and small rips. Dark fumes hissed from the muffler. Out of the corner of her eye, Jesse saw Lauren pinch her nose shut. The dust on the windows clouded Jesse's view of the driver, but she could see that he stared out the window at the trailer and Starbuck's rump that showed above the half door. The car nosed even with her and Lauren, and the driver twisted his head to stare at them, too. Jesse squirmed. She didn't like him looking at her. Or Lauren. Or Starbuck.

He smiled and waved at her and Lauren. Jesse flinched, but she had no reason to not like this man just because he stared. Alot of people liked to look at horses and often stopped to admire them. She smiled and gave a small wave back.

The car stopped next to the gas pump, between Jesse, Lauren and the trailer. The driver's door creaked open and the driver stepped out facing the trailer. His dark hair hung long and greasy in a ponytail that hung down the back of an old dapple green hunting coat. He began to pump gas into his car. Only then did he pivot his head to glance back at her. His thin lips stretched over a wide mouth and his nose had a twist to one side. His dark eyes drilled right into Jesse.

"That guy gives me the creeps," Lauren whispered. She tugged on Jesse's arm. "Come on, let's go back inside and get some chips or somethin' till your dad comes."

Jesse scolded herself as they half-walked half-ran back to the store. Was she going to imagine every man they saw that looked at her or Starbuck might be the thief? She needed to get a life. Still, that guy creeped her out, too.

They found Jesse's dad in the rear of the station, talking with the service mechanic about an old rusting Buick parked on the side. Several minutes later, when they went out the front of the store, the old Plymouth had left.

Lauren leaned close to Jesse in the truck. "Gas Card."

"Yep."

The Lauren made a face and rolled her eyes at Jesse. "Creepy."

"Very."

As they drove, Jesse checked the side-mirror at the road behind them. Once she thought she saw the Plymouth behind them, three cars back. Then, another car wedged between them in the lineup, and she lost sight of it. When she could finally see the cars behind them again, there was no Plymouth. It had to be a coincidence. The highway only went two ways. There was fifty-fifty chance the driver of the Plymouth would be headed their way. She'd have to get a grip on herself. She checked the mirror every few minutes for the rest of the ride.

A few hours later they turned down the long road that led past the Saucier's stable and their own home into Caribou. No Plymouth had followed them. She laughed at herself. What a spook.

Her dad swung the truck and trailer into the Saucier's drive. Lauren's parents came out of their big brick house as Lauren ran to give them a hug. Jesse crawled out of the truck and stretched her sore muscles. She hobbled over to Lauren's parents with her father.

"Barry. Ramona." Jesse's dad shook hands with Lauren's parents. "Wondered if you had an extra stall we could keep Starbuck in for awhile."

Lauren's father answered, "Anything you need, Ray. I'll make room in the stall right next to Lauren's horse." Lauren raised her eyebrows and flashed a wide grin at Jesse and raced to the barn.

"That'll be fine, thanks."

While the Sauciers readied the stall, Jesse and her dad went to get Starbuck from the trailer. Jesse stood on tiptoe and kissed her dad on the cheek. "Thanks Dad."

CHAPTER 16

Monday afternoon, Jesse stepped into her fifth stall of the day and began to rake through the shavings with her pick. She really didn't mind cleaning stalls, and she wanted to help with Starbuck's boarding bill, but some of these horses were just plain disgusting. She lifted the pick and scraped it against the dried manure on the wall. Bits of the crusty material crumbled off and onto the pile beneath it. She sighed and pulled her scraper from her hip pocket, propping her pick against the wall.

"So you found Starbuck?" Stacey's voice came from behind Jesse.

Jesse didn't looked up from her task. She wedged the tip of the scraper under a clump and pried. "Yep."

"Well, I'm glad. Lauren told me you even caught one of the thieves, but the other one is still loose. Has the one in jail said anything yet?"

"Not yet." The dried chunk peeled off and slid to the floor. Jesse wiped the scraper on the foot of her boot and tucked it back into her pocket.

Stacey didn't say anything more. A trickle of sweat

rolled into Jesse's eyes and she swiped at it with the shoulder of her already wet shirt. She reached for her pick.

Stacey spoke again. "Lauren says you're not going to ride in the Classic."

"No. There's not enough time."

Stacey's voice seemed to relax. "I think you're doing the right thing, with the Classic only a week away. I wouldn't compete either, if it was me."

Jesse nodded.

"Well, congratulations on finding him."

"Yep."

After a moment, Jesse heard Stacey's footsteps walk away from the door of the stall. Jesse turned around and rested the tines of the pick on the floor, watching Stacey walk down the alley and out the front door. What had that been about? Was she trying to make up? Jesse snorted. Stacey most likely was trying to figure out if she had a chance in the competition.

Jesse looked around the stall. She had enough time to finish this one and one more before she quit to go home. A solid brown stain stretched all the way around the stall, dotted with patches of dried manure. No one had done a good job cleaning this stall in a long time. She set down her pick, pulling her scraper out again. There would be no other stall today. In fact, this stall might be a two-day project. Animals always reflected their owners. That was the theory. If that was true, she didn't want to think much on the habits of the owner of this horse. She tried to shove the point of the scraper under the nearest patch, but the manure was dried tightly to the wall.

Jesse yawned. Last night she'd had her nightmare again. This time though, the man at the gas station became the man at the door in her nightmare. He'd climbed out of his rusted green Plymouth and walked to the door, cowboy-style spurs sparking on the sidewalk. It was Jesse and not her mother who opened the door. Again the man chased her, and again she'd become Starbuck. Then she woke up in a sweat-drenched bed. She stayed awake the rest of the night, like the night before that, and the night before that even. It seemed like she had the nightmare every time she fell asleep. At least Starbuck was safe and in a place that would keep an eye on him twenty-four hours a day. Maybe she'd go to bed early tonight.

As if on cue, Jesse's watch alarm began to beep. Surprised, she checked the time. An hour had passed while she'd been working on the same patch. She grabbed her pick and walked out of the stall. She couldn't get the bedding wet with water, but maybe a small spray bottle wouldn't hurt too much. She'd try that tomorrow.

When Jesse joined her father in the house, she found him standing in front of the television with the clicker in his hand. He glanced up at her and said, "Jess, come here. Look at this."

The TV showed firefighters in the dark of night battling against a huge structural fire. The light from the flames made the nearby trees dance like demons. Men in heavy coats trained fire hoses onto the blaze, while others worked in front of their trucks. Suddenly, an explosion belched out of the building as part of the roof caved in. A news commentator cut off the scene. "This picture happened at four o'clock this morning at the main barn of international horse trainer, Bob Jenson. The cause is as yet undetermined, but arson hasn't been ruled out. Killed in the fire were seven horses and one firefighter. Services for the firefighter will be held –"

Jesse's dad turned off the volume and reached for

the phone. He dialed, and then, after a minute, said, "Hello? Bob? ... Oh, John. This is Ray Marsh. Anything we can do? ... I've got room for one or two here. ... All right. They'll be ready." When he hung up he said to Jesse, "Most of the horses are going back home to their owners. Bob has a couple of his own horses that are needing a place for awhile. We've got that empty stall, and I thought we could put one in Starbuck's stall, unless you want him home."

She shook her head. "No. That's fine. I'll leave him there."

He hesitated, searching her eyes. Then he said, "You can keep him there as long as you want. I just want to make sure you understand that there was nothing you did wrong that caused him to be stolen."

Jesse bit her lip, and her eyes filled with tears. He pulled her into his arms, stroking her hair. "Hey, it's not your fault. Honest. Sometimes these things happen, even when you do everything right."

"I know. That's what scares me. What if it happens again? What if something worse happens?"

"Sometimes really bad things happen that we have no control over. That's part of life. It's okay to be scared. But you can't live the rest of your life that way. That's not living. The best you can do is to try to protect yourself and the ones you love, and be ready in case something bad does happen."

"I don't want something bad to happen!"

"I know. Neither do I." He held her until her tears settled to sniffles. Then he said, "Better now? Do you understand that it had nothing to do with you?"

She nodded. "Yes."

"Do you want to help me get the stalls ready? Jenson's horses will be here in an hour. They're taking a couple to Saucier's too."

She burst out laughing. "The stalls are ready. I keep them that way, because Lauren puts Legs in there sometimes. We just need to get fresh water and hay out for them."

CHAPTER 17

Mid-morning, the next day, Jesse scanned the Jockey Club's website for information on how to find a thoroughbred's owner. The American Stud Book Online had what she wanted, but it cost $150 to join. Not likely. She only needed one pedigree. She could hire a pedigree research company for $35. $50 would give her the breeder's name. That would take weeks. Another website listed pedigrees for free. But they didn't have Kula's pedigree because she hadn't raced. She stared at the tattoo number and drummed her fingertips on her desktop, lips pursed. P41473. The P told her that Kula had been born in 1985. They still printed the hard copy of the American Stud Book in 1985. She snapped off her computer. She'd have to go a different route to find out what she wanted.

She called Lauren. "Hey, you want to go to the library at the university? Dad will probably take us to Drizzo's for lunch if we can get there by noon." She held her breath. "They have the most wonderful cinnamon ice cream, remember?"

"We gonna go on our bikes?"

Jesse grinned to herself and glanced out the window

at the brilliant blue sky. Not a single cloud. "Yeah, unless we can hitch a ride with somebody from the stable."

"I'll check."

Jesse hung up and settled back in her chair at the kitchen table to wait for Lauren. That morning's newspaper lay in front of her. She rustled through it and glanced over the photos of the fire. Several photos showed the tiny crowd gathered to help the Jensens save the horses.

In the background of one photo, behind almost everyone, stood Roberta Michaud. Emotional shock traced through Jesse's fingertips and sent chills up her spine. She snatched up the paper and held it close. Jesse's heart pounded. Why was Roberta there? She lived too far away to even think of getting there in time to help. The TV report said it was a flash fire, over and burnt to the ground in no time.

She fumbled with the pages and tore a long slit across the middle of one, before she found the end of the article again. No Michauds in the list of horse owners. Not even Roberta's maiden name, Ramsey, was listed. She rechecked the names of the horses themselves, but again found nothing familiar. Maybe Roberta showed up to see what cleanup she could do. Was that it? She held the paper up close to her eyes, to look for Stacey.

"You need glasses?"

Startled, Jesse dropped the paper and banged her knee against the table leg. She jerked her head up and saw Lauren laughing from the doorway. Roberta Michaud smiled from behind her.

Jesse flushed and bent to pick up the paper. She needed to clear the blush from her face. Her heart hammered a staccato in her chest. She played for time and pretended to fumble at the paper. She said from her upside down angle, "You found a ride."

"I told you I'd check. Get movin', or she'll leave us behind."

Jesse snatched the paper and straightened. Her face still felt warm, but at least now she had an excuse. She rose to her feet. "Let me just put this away, and I'll meet you outside."

"Cute place." Roberta walked around Lauren and into the kitchen. She didn't seem to notice Jesse's face, or even that Jesse took a step backwards away from her as she came close. "I thought I might buy a small place like this."

"Um, thanks. It's comfortable." Jesse felt tense with Roberta in her kitchen. She wadded the paper into fourths and threw it on top of the refrigerator. "I'll get that later, let's go." She dodged past Roberta and Lauren to wait with her hand on the doorknob. Maybe Roberta would take the hint.

Lauren pivoted on her heel and clunked down the stairs. Roberta viewed the room once more and then followed. Jesse held her breath as the woman passed. She debated with herself about whether to lock the door or not. She and her dad never did. She felt a little foolish, but Roberta unnerved her. She felt like she needed to lock her out of her life. At least from her mind. She twisted the key in the ancient lock face.

Roberta's Escalade roared to life and she sped them toward town. Her perfume billowed throughout the vehicle until Jesse felt she would choke. The yellow broken lines in the center of the road flipped by with alacrity. Trees filled the roadside and shadows from them matched the speed of the yellow lines. Jesse stared out the window at them until they flew around a pair of potato trucks also on the way to town.

Roberta pulled back into their lane and spoke. "Lauren, you're riding in the Classic, right?"

"Absolutely. Legs is in top form."

"What about you, Jesse? I'll be there with Esquibar."

Jesse didn't like Roberta's Thoroughbred. No one could handle him. The horse had a reputation as a hothead. The last time she'd seen Roberta ride him, Esquibar had bulled right through a jump. He didn't even try to go over or evade it. He'd splintered the wood like it had been matchsticks. Lauren's dad had thought of buying him until that incident. Now Roberta couldn't find a buyer anywhere. She turned to Roberta. "I saw your picture in the paper. At the fire, I mean."

"I couldn't sleep and when I heard the news. I just had to go help." An opening in the trees let the sunlight stream in through the windshield. Roberta squinted and reached up to adjust the visor. She didn't seem to notice that Jesse didn't answer her question.

"Did Stacey go, too? I didn't see her picture."

Roberta's squint turned to a frown and she shook her head, "No. She said she didn't feel well when she went to bed. I just left her asleep at home and went by myself."

"What do you suppose caused the fire?"

Roberta twisted her head to regard Jesse. Her hazel eyes turned hard and swept back and forth across Jesse's face. She seemed to want to see inside Jesse, as if she could read her mind. Then she turned back to the road and said, "Nobody knows. I think it had something to do with his tractor, though. Do you know he parks it in the end stall of the barn? I would never do that. I value my horses too much."

They returned to the silence that had begun the trip

and Jesse almost whistled with relief when she opened the car door in front of the green cinder block Aroostook County Farm Bureau building. Jesse didn't see her dad anywhere in the Soil Conservancy office, so she wandered down the hall to his secretary. Lauren followed behind.

"You dad's just down the hall, honey, he'll be right back. Why don't you wait in his office?"

When they had settled into her father's two brown vinyl chairs, she leaned over to Lauren and asked, "Don't you think it's odd that Roberta went to that fire?"

"No. She just wanted to help. I would have if I'd been awake."

"Yeah, but the fire was at three thirty in the morning. Why do you think she was awake?"

Lauren shrugged and picked up the copy of Potato Farmer Magazine from the end table. The cover showed a planter silhouetted against a giant orange sun. "Who knows?" She gazed at the cover for a moment and then tossed it back.

"You don't think it's strange that she didn't take Stacey with her?"

"I don't know. She said Stacey didn't feel well." Lauren shifted in her chair so she could stare past the end table and out the window.

Jesse didn't say anything. When Lauren talked about it like that, it all seemed to make sense.

"There are my girls." Jesse's dad walked in with a giant grin. "Are you hungry? Do you want to go to Drizzo's?"

CHAPTER 18

After eating lunch at Drizzo's, Jesse's dad dropped them off at the Mid-Maine Community College library after lunch. "I'll be back in an hour." Then he drove off.

Jesse liked the campus. She thought the faded brickwork and green tarnished copper roofs added an amiable atmosphere to Caribou. Milton Library sat right in the middle and all the dorms and classroom buildings ringed around it, like the hub of a wheel. A bridge angled across a tiny stream halfway to the Student Union. Sometimes, in the summer, she wandered down to the bridge and spent the day with a book. Maybe if they had time, they could do that. For now, though, they had to climb to the very topmost floor and trek to the very back corner of the Agri-science section in order to find what she wanted.

Lauren disappeared down the aisle and around the corner. The American Stud Books sat on the very bottom shelf, right next to the fire exit. Jesse squatted and pulled the volume that said '1985'. She stood and walked to a tiny cubicle against the window. A window branched above the desk and she could see students, with low-slung backpacks, trudge to other buildings. What would it feel like when she became a college student? She couldn't imagine it.

She blew the dust off the top edge of her book, set it flat and lifted the cover. 1985. The year of Kula. She giggled out loud, and then looked around to see if anyone had noticed. Nobody looked up from the other cubicles. She paged through the book until she found it. 41473. Enspirited Design. No doubt misspelled on purpose. She liked the name Kula better. She reached for a slip of scratch paper and one of the chewed on pencils. Born January first. A lot of horses claimed that, but she knew that quite a few Thoroughbred breeders foaled their mares in the prior December. A bigger foal sold and raced better. Breeder: Susan Batelle of Illinois. By the 1976 stallion Spirit de Corps. Out of the 1980 mare Flighty Design. It confirmed that Kula had never raced. She'd have to go to the 1976 and 1980 volumes for more of the pedigree. She whispered Kula's registered name. Thoroughbred names felt magic in her mouth. They had a secret power, like the wind. She thumbed through a few pages and tried the names she came across.

Lauren came up beside her and brandished a book in front of her, "Hey, have you read this?" Then she dropped her hand, fingers splayed, onto the Stud Book on the table. "Esquibar."

Jesse shook her head. "No. It says here it's a horse named Naziah."

"Those are Esquibar's bloodlines. I know them. I studied them when Dad thought about buying him last year."

"Wrong year. Must be a brother."

"Must be. You know, that name sounds familiar." Lauren stared down at Jesse with a puzzled frown. Then she snapped her fingers. "I think he," and she pointed to

Naziah's page, "was in Jensen's barn."

Roberta's horse's brother. It made sense that Roberta would be at the fire. Jesse glanced up at the breeder's name. Joseph Hyatt of Florida. She stood and retraced her path through the aisles and down the stairs to the periodicals. It only took a minute for her to find the Caribou paper and return to Lauren. "Look, he's one of the ones that died. It says Joseph Hyatt still owned him." Was there a connection between Roberta and this Joseph? Or was it just a coincidence?

Jesse scribbled down the registry information for Naziah and returned the book to the shelf while Lauren pulled the volumes for Kula's sire and dam. The books showed that both had raced, so she could get the rest of the pedigree online if she needed. It would be quicker that way. The priority, though, was to find Kula's owners. She slammed the books shut and she and Lauren reshelved them. Then they jogged down the steps to the computer room.

Jesse settled into a chair, and pulled up the people search engine. Lauren said, "I'm thirsty. Hurry up so we can get something from the Student Union before your dad comes back."

Jesse looked up from the monitor. "Go ahead. I don't know how long this is going to take."

Lauren nodded. "Okay. I'll get you a pop, too." Then she left.

Jesse turned back to the computer and typed in Susan Batelle. Nothing came up for that name, but there was a S. Batelle in Brighton, Illinois. She clicked on that and then scribbled down the phone number, email, and address. Then she typed in Joseph Hyatt.

The search engine brought up the information on Joseph immediately, including links to four recent news articles. He still lived in Florida. Orlando, to be exact. Why would a Florida horse be in Caribou, and at the burning barn Roberta drove to in the middle of the night, when she lived on the other side of town? They had to be connected somehow. She wrote Joseph's contact information under Susan's and clicked on the link that said, "Hyatt Does It Again!"

The newspaper article was written only three days ago. Joseph Hyatt seemed to be not only a Thoroughbred breeder, but also a racehorse trainer. One of his colts had taken the deluxe Breeder's Stakes in South Carolina. Why would a racehorse trainer have a horse in a dressage trainer's barn? Perhaps Roberta was leasing him, or trying him out with the thought of buying him. That gave her the reason to be at the barn in the middle of the night. But then, why hadn't she just said that? Why would she keep it all a secret? Jesse shook her head. It must be some horse, to rate Jensen's barn. Roberta was probably planning to surprise everyone with her new horse at the Classic. It would give her the edge.

Jesse glanced at her watch. She still had fifteen minutes before her dad came. Looking around, she saw that Lauren was still gone. Jesse logged into her email server and began an email to Susan Batelle.

"Is that Kula's owner?" Lauren's voice came from close behind her. A bolt of adrenalin zinged through Jesse. She jumped and her elbow knocked against the table.

She laughed, rubbing her elbow. "I just looked for you, and you weren't there. I didn't hear you come up behind me."

Lauren grinned and handed her a diet Coke. "Yup, you looked pretty into your email."

"That's Kula's breeder. I figure she might know

who owns Kula now, if she doesn't."

Lauren read the email out loud. "'Dear Ms. Batelle. I have recently come across a stolen mare named "Enspirited Design".' You misspelled that."

"No, that's the way the book has it."

"Huh." Lauren continued. "'I am currently searching for her current owners. If you can help me, please email me back, or contact Detective Lowrey of the Caribou Police Department. His phone number follows.' You're always so polite. I wouldn't know what to say." She slurped on her pop and turned her head toward the window. "Your dad's here."

Jesse typed in Dectective Lowrey's phone number and clicked the send button. As soon as she got the confirmation that the email had been sent, she turned off the computer and joined Lauren walking to her Dad's truck.

By the time they got home, Jesse had a return email from Susan Batelle. "The information I have is a couple years old. When I tried their phone number, I found it disconnected. There was no information on the internet. I'm sorry. I've also given your Detective Lowrey this information. He seems very impressed with you and told me the general story of what happened. Good Job!!! If there's anything I can do, let me know."

Jesse sputtered her lips in frustration. Now what?

CHAPTER 19

Wednesday morning, Jesse's sat on Starbuck about 10 feet away from the edge of the arena. She shortened her left reign, flexing Starbuck's head to the left, and shifted her weight to her left hip. Then she nudged him at the cinch with her left leg. As he started to turn to the left, she brought her right leg in against him. She didn't want him to turn in a circle. She wanted him to shift his hindquarters to the right. She slid her left leg even further back toward his flank, exaggerating the cue to show him what she wanted him to move. His answer was to arch his neck, throw his shoulder forward to the right, step forward, and turn a circle to the left. Jesse stopped him and dropped her reins. She stared at Lauren. "That's all he wants to do. Why? What's wrong with what I'm telling him?"

Lauren sat on Legs, watching from the center of the arena, her eyes squinted against the sunlight. "Nothing. He knows that cue. I've seen him do it for you before. He just doesn't want to do it. He's bullying you."
Jesse nodded and then sighed. "Yeah, I know. It's just...."
She let her voice fade. It was just that she was still scared.

"Maybe you ought to change your work out. Instead

of just dressage, why don't you take him through Jump Alley?"

Jesse sat up in the saddle and shaded her eyes against the sun. She could just see long thin fenced runway from here. Three horses grazed at odd angles in between two of the jumps. One of them must have balked at the monster shaped standards she and Lauren had built over the winter. The riders had dismounted and were working to open one of the escape gates between the jumps.

"Same rules as always." Lauren said.

"No gates." Jesse considered it. Once they'd started, they'd have to ride it to the end. Since the jumps ran the full width of the Alley, neither of them could avoid a jump, unless the rider admitted defeat and used an escape gate. It used to be their most favorite ride. On a good day, Starbuck could blow Legs away. On a bad day, Legs would stretch out and leave Starbuck to choke on her dust. They hadn't used the gates in months.

The three riders in the Alley had tugged their horses through the gate and began to remount. It looked like they planned to try the Alley again. Jesse shook her head and turned Starbuck back to the corner of the arena where she'd been working him. "It looks pretty busy, I think we'll just stay here. I've got to get this darned Turn on the Forehand down."

"Come on Jesse! It'll be fun! Who cares if there are people there already, there's always enough room."

"Nah, I'd rather work alone with him right now."

All at once, she felt her saddle lurch sideways at the same time two arms reached around her waist and took hold of the reins. Behind her, she felt Lauren bump her calves aginst Starbuck's flank. Then Lauren turned him around and began to canter toward the jumps, Legs in tow. "Let me remind you why you began showing in the first place."

Jesse laughed the whole way to the start of Jump Alley.

Lauren bailed off onto her own horse and said, "You first."

Jesse eyed the jumps. They did look fun. The other riders were just coming around behind them to go again.

Suddenly, Lauren and Legs bolted past them. "Last one through gets to brush out all the water buckets tomorrow!" Lauren craned her neck over her shoulder and flashed a wicked grin at Jesse.

Jesse shuddered and dug her heels into Starbuck's sides. Cleaning the buckets was a nasty job, especially alone. Jesse raised up in her stirrups and leaned low over Starbuck's whithers. The race was on!

She hopped Starbuck over the first two low red-spiral painted rails. Jesse saw that Lauren had reached the short oxer and had launched Legs over the shorter front rail toward the taller rail in back. Starbuck felt like a bundle of energy underneath Jesse, and he pulled at the reins to catch up with Legs. He sailed over the oxer without a single tip or knock.

By the time Jesse and Starbuck reached the next jump, the double combination with the painted cut out monsters on the sides, she'd almost caught Lauren. Starbuck tensed himself to follow Legs over the first half of the jump. The sound of his hooves striking the ground stopped as he lifted into the air. Jesse began to count: Jump-stride one-stride two-jump. Then they sailed across the second half of the jump and charged on to the 'brick' wall.

Lauren snuck a peek behind her, to check on Jesse. She frowned when she saw Jesse so close. Lauren leaned next to Legs. The sound of her voice whipped back in the air to Jesse.

Jesse leaned closer to Starbuck, kissing at him to speed up. A sudden jolt coursed through her as he leapt forward. She smiled. They were still gaining.

Lauren sailed over the wall jump, and landed just as Jesse launched Starbuck into it. The fake potted plants flashed by on either side of Jesse. Then she and Lauren splashed side by side through the water jump, hopping over the row of tires half way through. Then they were on to the last jump.

Lauren began to shout at Legs, and her horse surged forward again. Those long Thoroughbred legs ate up the ground. She'd already landed on the other side of the tall gate jump when Jesse began.

Starbuck launched himself upwards, and for a moment they were flying. Jesse closed her eyes. All sound disappeared, except the wind and the sound of her horse drawing a breath. Then his front feet touched down on the other side and he gusted out in a great whoosh of air. Jesse felt his shoulder muscles give and rebound with the shock of the impact of landing. Then he stretched his front legs forward and raced toward Legs. Jesse opened her eyes and sat up. Ahead, Lauren dropped her reins, and threw her arms up in a victory sign. Legs slowed to a trot as Starbuck cantered up beside her. Jesse caught Lauren's eye, and they both laughed, slapping their horses' necks. Lauren's face was flush from the excitement and Jesse's felt the same. Together, they chattered about the upcoming Classic as they rode back to the barn.

By the time her dad pulled up to take her home, Jesse felt like her old self again. She waved goodbye to Lauren, piled into the truck, and kissed her dad on the cheek.

"Well, it looks like you had fun today," he said as he turned the truck for home.

"Oh, Dad, we did!" Jesse described the race to him. The excitement of the story made her feel breathless and giddy. "Dad, I've decided to ride in the Classic."

CHAPTER 20

The day of the show, Jesse and her father pulled into the stable parking lot at five in the morning. Lauren's father looked up from under the hood of their work truck and gave a wry smile to Jesse's dad. Then he waved at Jesse as she ran to the barn.

Inside the barn, six voices shouted at each other from behind closed stall doors. Giggles came right after. Mixed with the smell of hay, came leather oil, Vetrolin and shampoo. A stall door scraped open and a petite dark-haired girl carrying a hot pink mounting block stepped out. A pair of scissors clattered to the floor from her carpenter's apron.

"Let me get those for you, Polly." Jesse stooped to retrieve the fallen scissors and handed them to her friend.

Polly laughed. "I don't know don't know which way I'm goin' anymore! I've already braided three horses this morning, but I've still got two to go!" She scurried away, and slipped into another stall.

Jesse found Lauren in Legs stall, fussing over Legs' two white hind stockings. Legs ignored the work at her feet and chewed the remains of her grain.

"Jesse! I'm so glad you're finally here! Do her legs look white to you? They look kinda yellow to me yet.

127

What do you think?" Lauren frowned and stepped back to survey the offending socks.

"They look pretty snowy to me," Jesse answered. "No matter how blinding white those stockings become, they won't be white enough for you." She laughed.

Lauren stuck her tongue out at Jesse and squatted down with her box of baking soda and brush.

Jesse grinned and then left for Starbuck's stall. Easing in, she saw Starbucks mane in a tiny row of braids, each one as perfect as the other. No hairs escaped, and they spaced evenly all the way down his neck. His tail and forelock even had smooth braids in them. Jesse hadn't thought to hire Polly to braid Starbuck. She hadn't even thought that far ahead.

Starbuck left his breakfast and turned his head to whuffle his nose in her palm. The fine soft hairs around his mouth whispered across her hand and up her arm. Jesse laughed. "I didn't bring any treats for you. You're supposed to be eating your breakfast."

Starbuck turned his attention her jeans pockets, bumping her while he searched. Jesse's breath caught in her throat. How close they came to not being here at all today.

Satisfied that there were no treats to be had, Starbuck returned to his hay, jerking giant mouthfuls from the rack. Jesse leaned against his solid body, and pressed her cheek against his neck. She couldn't quite get into the mood of the day. It used to be that she would holler back and forth with every one else while they all groomed their horses, laughing and giggling. She thought today would be fun and she'd be happy, but now she wasn't so sure. Maybe she made a mistake signing up for the show.

Sighing, she pulled out a brush out of her back pocket. It had crimped from the ride in the truck, but it would work. She reached up and ran the brush down Starbucks smooth neck, watching the tracks it made in his shiny coat. It soothed something inside her.

Just then, Polly ducked her head into the stall. "Was it alright that I did him? I just thought you might like the help, with everything that's been going on and all. It's on the house. I don't want any money for it." She fidgeted and looked uncertain.

Jesse grinned. "Thanks Polly, he looks great. I appreciate it."

Polly flashed a pearly white smile and then vanished.

Jesse returned her attention to Starbuck. Maybe it would be good for her to go. It might get her back into the swing of her old life again. Picking up her spray bottle, she inspected his coat. He'd had a bath yesterday, but she was sure he still had stains. She sprayed her special mix of Vetrolin and rubbing alcohol on a spot and then scrubbed with her rag. The medicine smell of the mix stung her nose. "Smelly stuff," she told Starbuck. When she'd cleaned enough spots, she began to wrap his legs for the drive.

At seven-thirty the two trailers pulled out of the drive. Jesse, her father and Lauren pulled the three-horse slant trailer with Starbuck, Legs and Polly's little roan mare, Bint Syrah inside. The drive from the stable to the show grounds seemed like forever to Jesse, even though they were going just a few miles south of Presque Isle. Lauren kept up a constant gab about anything that popped into her head. Jesse did her best to be good company, but her stomach knotted-up at the thought of being in front of all those people. She used to love showing. Had her fear done this? She pressed her lips in a thin line and frowned. No more. Her dad was right. Everyone was right. She wasn't going to let fear control her life.

By the time they reached the fairgrounds and began unloading the horses, Jesse felt more lighthearted than she had since Starbuck had been stolen. Roberta's matching four-horse rig was parked in front of the doors to their assigned barn. She'd left no room for anyone else to bring a horse through. They all dismounted from the trucks, and Barry Saucier and Jesse's father walked into the barn, while Jesse and Lauren went to the trailer to get the horses ready to be unloaded.

While Lauren dropped the tailgate into place as a loading ramp, Jesse waited by the windows.

Stacey's voice floated to her from the end of the trailer where Lauren was. "I see Jesse decided to show after all. How stupid! Why didn't you talk her out of it?"

Lauren laughed. "Talk her out of it? I had to talk her into it."

"What kind of a friend are you? You know she won't show well. I'll beat her so badly, she'll be humiliated in front of all those people."

Jesse felt her face flame, and she started toward the back of the trailer.

Lauren's voice turned hard. "It seems to me that you're happy Starbuck was stolen. That's the only reason you'll beat her. Otherwise, she could tromp you any day, and you know it. If you don't mind, I'm busy with my *friend* now." She came around the side of the trailer, almost colliding with Jesse, her face dark with a scowl. She grabbed Jesse's arm and tugged her back toward the front of the trailer. "That Stacey burns me up! I'm done with her!"

Jesse let herself be pulled away from Stacey. Jesse smiled. "Thanks for what you told her."

Lauren shrugged "It's true. And I think you can still

take her in the jump classes. Now let's get these horses unloaded so we can prove it."

One-by-one they backed the horses out of the trailer and led them into stalls in the barn, the horse's shoes ringing on the cement aisle. Jesse rinsed the water buckets and filled them, while Lauren spread shavings on the floor. Polly brought hay in nets and strung them up in the stalls for the three horses.

"All done?" Lauren asked. "I'm gonna brush Legs really quick, then we can go watch the competition."

Jesse nodded. "Ok. I just need to get my soft brush. I left it on the trailer fender." She jogged down the aisle and out to the far side of the trailer. Her brush wasn't there. She eased onto her hands and knees, wincing at the sharp stabs of the rocks digging into her skin. Scanning under the trailer, but she didn't see it there either. She stood, wiping her hands on her jeans, dislodging little rocks and looking around. Nothing was on the ground. Where was her brush? Then she walked around the back of the trailer and looked inside. Nothing. She went up to the truck. Other than the flies that buzzed past when she looked in through the open window, the truck was empty.

She must have taken it inside with her. As she walked back to the barn, she scanned the ground in all directions. She pulled open Starbuck's stall and scuffed around in the shavings, but there was no brush. She frowned. She could use one of Lauren's brushes, but where was hers? She knew she'd last used it at the trailer to brush Starbuck's face. Was she crazy now, too?

CHAPTER 21

"Seventeen! Number 17! Please report to the warm-up arena! Number 17 please!" The loudspeaker boomed over the crowd.

Jesse glanced over at Lauren who was working Legs on dressage in the corner of the arena, a big seventeen pinned to Lauren's back. They were next. First Lauren and Legs and then Jesse and Starbuck. Jesse's stomach flip-flopped. She gritted her teeth. She'd worked a lot of hours before, and a little after, Starbuck's kidnapping to get ready for this show. She didn't expect to win. But she did want to place, and she wanted to place higher than Stacey who'd had a very impressive run. She wanted Lauren to win.

Starbuck squealed, shaking his head. His excitement almost pulled her over his neck. Glancing up, she saw her father standing beside the rail, her grandparents and Haley beside him. Jesse rode over to greet them.

"He looks excited, Jess," her father said, and he grabbed for the bridle.

"He is. Hi Haley." She smiled at the reporter, and then she waved to her grandparents.

"Hi Jesse. I heard you were riding today, so I

thought I'd come watch. It'd make a great follow up to your story. We're still getting calls at the paper about you."

"Really?"

"Uh Huh. People all the time want to know what happened to that nice young girl that had her horse stolen." Haley said and she reached over the rail and patted Starbuck on the shoulder.

The loudspeaker announced Lauren's number and Jesse turned Starbuck to give the thumb's up sign to her friend. Lauren moved to the gate. Just before she went in she turned and stuck her tongue out at Jesse. Then she smiled and cantered into the show arena.

Legs' long strides made the sound of her footfall seem casual as she warmed up. Then she glided through the first three jumps, all low singles. She started to pick up speed as she approached the oxer, but made the jump with room to spare. By the time they reached the next combination, Lauren had her back in control, and her hoof beats had once again settled into a slow rhythm.

Jesse turned her attention back to Starbuck for a moment, trying to calm his fussing. When she looked up, Lauren was almost through the course, with only two jumps left, a parallel and another oxer. The parallel she took well, clearing it easily, and then she was over the last oxer, too.

Jesse dropped her reins to join the crowd in applauding her friend's ride. Legs hadn't knocked or even tipped a single rail. Lauren's face beamed as she left the gate.

The loudspeaker announced Jesse's number.

"Go get 'em Jess!" Her grandfather patted her leg as her father turned Starbuck toward the gate.

Haley smiled and said, "Give me a story! Good luck!"

Jesse laughed. Starbuck rocked back and forth like a toy horse. Jesse forced her legs to relax and hang loose, to think limp and quiet. The trick worked and Starbuck began to calm down. Jesse moved him toward the arena gate. Just as she reached it she saw a man standing there. He looked like that man at the gas station. He had the same sideways twisted nose, but his ponytail had been cut off. This time he wore a striped short-sleeve shirt. He didn't smile at her like the rest of the crowd. His dark eyes seemed to stab right into her.

Starbuck pranced sideways and Jesse glanced down at her mount. He tried to bolt into the arena. She circled him once. When she looked back up at the gate, a different man stood there, smiling. She searched the crowd, and even stood in her stirrups to get a better look. The man with the crooked nose had disappeared. The loudspeaker boomed the last call for her.

She rode Starbuck into the arena. Had she been seeing things? She glanced back over her shoulder to check once again, but there was still no sign of the menacing figure. Jesse shook her head, trying to clear her thoughts. She must have been imagining it. She needed to concentrate on Starbuck and the jump course.

She cued Starbuck to pick up a canter for the warm up circle. He hesitated and flicked his ears back and forth. She needed to relax. She thought wet towel again, trying to make her legs heavy and limp. Her mind slipped back to the man at the gate. He couldn't have been real. He disappeared too fast.

Jesse cued Starbuck a second time. Again he hesitated, but then he lifted into a rough canter and took his circle. She felt tense, and she knew Starbuck felt it, too. "Relax, relax, relax," she whispered to herself.

They took the first three singles, and almost didn't clear the last of them. The oxer rose up ahead of them and Jesse tried to focus on her task. She needed to be there for Starbuck. She tried to measure the distance to the jump. They were off step. She squeezed the reins, and then realized she'd pulled him in too much and bumped him with her legs.

Jesse felt Starbuck thrust himself up for the jump, leaving the ground much sooner than he should have. He reached forward, arching his neck to extend his jump. Then he landed with a grunt. Jesse heard a loud thump as the top rail fell to the ground behind them.

She steadied Starbuck. The combination was a tricky one. The second part held a small spread. Jump, one, two, jump. She misjudged the distance again, and Starbuck left the ground too late for the spread. He carried her across, but again knocked rails to the ground.

They hopped another low single, and then the tall parallel loomed next. Jesse took a deep breath to calm her nerves as they approached. She squinted her eyes and counted the distance. Twice. She steadied Starbuck and squeezed him into the jump. This time they cleared the rails. Then they were on the ground again and racing over the last oxer. Her distraction had cost them. They wouldn't even place. She'd never hear the end of it from Stacey, now. Jesse searched the crowd around the gate again as she exited, but the man with the crooked nose just wasn't there.

Once the class was over and the ribbons had been awarded, Jesse rode back to the barn and began to untack Starbuck. Stacey walked past the stall and waved her red ribbon. "You didn't even place. I told you not to come. Well, let's hope you do better in your dressage class. I could use a little competition."

"Congratulations." Jesse's voice sounded automatic and uncaring, even to her. Thank goodness Stacey hadn't stopped. Jesse couldn't imagine how horrible Stacey would be if she'd won instead of Lauren.

Jesse dropped her saddle in her tack trunk and picked up the brush she'd borrowed from Lauren. She frowned at Starbuck while she brushed. It wasn't that she hadn't even placed that bothered her. It was that guy. Why had she seen him? He'd disappeared awfully fast. Too fast. Had he even really been there? Did she imagine him? If he wasn't really there, was something really wrong with her?

Lauren's voice barged into her thoughts. "Are you about done? I'm famished and I want a hot dog. Hurry up already."

Jesse shrugged and put her brush down. She scolded herself for seeing things. There had been nobody there. Stress had made her see him. And worry over Starbuck. And fear. She felt like she had to keep watch everywhere to make sure Starbuck was still safe. She thought she would lose her mind. Of course, if she was crazy, then worrying about that guy wouldn't help because there was no guy, just her mind playing tricks. If, on the other hand, the guy was real, then he was gone and she didn't have to worry anymore. Either way, she vowed to not think about it. She ran to join Lauren.

The Sauciers met them at the hot dog stand, excited about Lauren's ribbon and full of news. "Polly won her dressage class," said Lauren's mom. "Oh, I know she only competes against her own best score. But, still, her score was better than some of the top riders in the area. Some of the other boarders and students have ribbons, too. Jesse, I'm sorry you didn't do well in your jump class, but with everything that's happened to you lately, it's wonderful you're here at all. Maybe you'll do better in your next class."

The group began to make their way through the grandstand to join Jesse's family and Haley. Once, when Jesse glanced behind her, she thought she saw the twisted nose guy again. Same striped shirt. Same dark hair. Still staring at her. She changed direction and began moving toward him. She had to know if he was real.

She kept her eyes on the man and squeezed down the row of seats. She stepped on someone's foot and turned to apologize. When she looked back to where the man had been, the seat was empty. She scanned the crowd in all directions. Nothing. No way could someone have disappeared that fast. No way. Now she knew it was her imagination.

CHAPTER 22

Two hours later, Jesse and Lauren returned to the barn. The dressage class would begin in another forty-five minutes, and they had to get the horses warmed up and limber again. As Jesse reached the stall, her cellphone chirped at her from inside her tack box. Snatching it up and flipping it open, she said, "Hello?" She wandered out to the truck to look for her soft brush again while she talked. It had to be there.

"Jesse? This is Bob Fellum. I just wanted to thank you again for finding my horse. He's doing well. The vet says that he might be well enough to show again in the winter training shows."

"You show?" A niggling suspicion began to build inside Jesse's mind. Could that be the connection? "Do you know Roberta Michaud?"

"Roberta? Now that's a name I haven't heard in a long time. She's actually the one who got me started in showing. She was married to my cousin. How is she? Still as hard-core as she used to be?"

"Your cousin?" As Jesse walked past the front of

the trailer, a movement caught her eye.

"Yeah, you might have heard of him actually. He's a big name in the racing world. Joseph Hyatt."

Jesse stopped walking, her breath stuck in her throat. Joseph Hyatt? The man who owned the horse in the Jenson's barn. Roberta's ex-husband. She knew Bob Fellum and his stolen horses. She and Stacey both competed against Jesse. She blinked her eyes and focused on the movement that had caught her attention earlier. A wire dangled from the emergency braking box. The loose end had been cut clean, the wires sharp and shiny. The cap of the brake battery compartment sat askew, and Jesse lifted it to peek in. The battery was gone.

If the trailer broke loose from the truck while traveling, it would have no emergency brakes to stop it. It would crash. The horses inside would get hurt, and maybe killed. Starbuck rode in that trailer.

"Jesse? You still there?"

"Um, yeah. Can I call you back? I'm at a show right now."

"You bet. If you see Roberta, give her my regards."

"Sure." Jesse turned off her phone and raced back into the barn to find one of the Sauciers. She found her father and Haley first. She quickly told them about her conversation with Bob and her suspicions. Then she told them about what she found at the trailer.

Her dad frowned and folded his lips into a tight line. He turned toward Legs's stall. "Lauren!"

When her face appeared, he said, "Go get your dad, right now. Hurry"

She hesitated, frowning. Then shut the door of the stall and ran out of the barn.

"Haley, stay here with Jesse while I check this out."

He returned ten minutes later with Lauren, his face anxious. "Well, it's definitely been cut. There are metal shavings under the hitch, too. Someone has tampered with that trailer. The other trailer's fine. Barry went after the police. I don't want anyone going anywhere alone."

"You think it's the other thief?" Haley asked.

"I think it could be."

Jesse froze. The picture of the twisted nose man flashed into her mind. "I think...I think I saw him," she said.

"You saw this guy?" her father asked.

"I saw someone who just stared at me. I saw him three different times, I think. I guess he could have been only a spectator," she paused, "but Lauren and I saw him on the road from Grandma's and Grandpa's house."

"Good, when the police get here, you need to tell them everything you can remember. I'm cancelling the rest of your rides. I'm calling Lowrey."

Jesse hugged herself. She thought she'd been going crazy. Her skin crawled when she pictured him. She glanced around her for the thief, just in case. A few of the crowd from the show came into the barn, but most hurried on their route and didn't stay long. A few still stood nearby in a tight group, talking. She didn't see the thief anywhere.

Barry Saucier and the head of show security arrived with three men. The security man listened while Jesse described what she knew about the situation, Roberta, and the man she'd seen. After she described the thief to him, he pointed to his men. One wore show clothes, but the other two wore street clothes. "These are my men. I've assigned them to follow each one of you while you're here. They are for your protection. If you," and he looked at Jesse and Lauren, "see the thief, let the police officer know. I'll arrange for a State police car to follow you on the trip home. I would like you all to take a good look at these men, so you can recognize them if you need them."

Or *when* I need them, Jesse thought.

Barry shook his head. "I'm canceling Lauren's ride, too. It's just too dangerous."

Lauren nodded. "There's always next year."

Jesse's dad said, "Detective Lowrey is going to meet us at the stable when we get back home. Why don't you and Lauren get changed while we wait for the rest of the group to show up."

Jesse nodded and she and Lauren grabbed their jeans, tee shirts, and street shoes. Outside the barn, they pushed their way through the crowd toward the women's room to change.

"I'm sorry about your not being able to ride."

Lauren slipped her arm around Jesse's. "No biggie. Friends stick together, right?" She leaned in close to Jesse and whispered, "Is he there?"

Jesse glanced behind her at their assigned guard. He paused at a nearby booth and picked up a toy lizard on a stick, pretending to play with it. His eyes scanned the crowd. When he saw her stare, he smiled.

"He's kinda cute." Lauren's voice filled Jesse's ear.

"He's not here to make friends."

"No, but he is cute. What do you suppose he'd do if we tried to ditch him?"

Jesse sighed and shook her head as she swung open the door to the ground level of the stadium. To Lauren this may be a game, but it was just plain scary to her. She intended to stay right where her guard could see her. A cheer broke loose in the stands above her. "Someone must have had a clean round of jumps."

"Like me."

"Yeah, only more advanced than you."

"Next year."

"Next year, you still won't be at that level. Maybe two years."

Lauren didn't answer. Instead she pivoted around to walk backwards. "He sure is cute."

"Stop it. He's supposed to be undercover." Jesse hissed. She shoved open the door to the bathroom and jerked Lauren in with her. Women packed the room. Jesse and Lauren angled to an empty corner.

Jesse tugged at her boots. They thunked to the floor one by one. She finished changing first and hollered to Lauren on her way out the door, "I'm going to wait out in the hall." Near our guard, she thought. Most of the women had emptied out by then, but she still didn't like to be far from help. She stepped out the door to wait.

The security guard had moved off down the hall. He stood with his back to the bathroom, his foot propped on the step at the water fountain. He picked at his fingernails with a small knife. He raised his head and peered ahead of him down the hallway. Then, he focused on his knife-work again.

A soft scrape sounded from one of the shadows between Jesse and the guard. A dark figure edged into the hallway, something shiny in his hand. It caught a small ray of light and flashed at her. A knife, long and jagged.

Lauren skidded out of the bathroom and slammed into Jesse's back. Neither of them said anything, but Lauren's hand closed on her elbow and she gasped. Jesse felt her eyes grow wide and her mouth opened into a scream, but no voice came with it.

The figure took a step toward them. His twisted

nose looked like a claw in the dim light. He waved the knife back and forth at them, then he half-turned his head toward the guard. His eyes never left Jesse. He smirked and then stepped back into the shadow again.

Down the hall, Jesse saw their guard shift and stand. He turned and faced them. A moment earlier and he would have seen the thief. Jesse pointed into the shadows where Riperton had disappeared.

The guard rushed over to them, drawing a gun from inside his show jacket with one hand and a radio with the other. To Jesse and Lauren, he said, "Stay with me." As he backed out of the building, pushing them behind him, he spoke on the radio. "We have a sighting on Riperton. Section C-7. I'm returning the girls to their barn."

By the time they managed to get through the crowd to the barn, the other security guards were calling in on the radio. No Riperton.

CHAPTER 23

The horse trailers pulled into the stable that night to find Detective Lowrey waiting. He said to Jesse, her father, and the Sauciers, "We've arrested Roberta Michaud. She confessed the whole thing. It seems Banks worked for her ex-husband. She hired him and Riperton to steal and kill her horses so she could collect insurance money on them. She collected on seven horses over the past five years, but she never got caught because they were different breeds and she insured them with different companies. The horse in the fire was still registered in her ex-husband's name, but she had transfer papers signed by him, so technically the horse was hers. One of those horses at your grandpa's, Jesse, is hers too. A mare named Enspirited Design."

Jesse's heart lurched. Kula was Roberta's? She didn't like that at all.

Her father spoke. "And she had other people's horses stolen and killed to make it look random?"

The detective nodded. "There was the added benefit of cutting down the show competition for her and Stacey. She says that she hasn't had any contact with Riperton since before the fire. She didn't tell him to sabotage your trailer.

That was his doing."

"So he's still on the loose, and playing his own game now?"

"That's about it." Detective Lowrey shook his head. He jabbed his finger at Jessie and Lauren, "You two don't go anywhere. Not anywhere. Not alone. Not at all. Get it?"

Jesse's father nodded and said, "I've already made that clear to them."

Detective Lowrey said. "We've got police everywhere and I've assigned a man to stay with each one of you in your houses. I've got a man who'll watch the barn, too. He won't get past us."

Barry Saucier spoke up. "Jesse, we'll take care of Starbuck and your things. Go on home."

Jesse's dad gripped her arm and pulled her to the truck. When they reached their house, she saw a blue squad car parked outside their house. A blond police officer exited the vehicle and walked into the house with them. "I'm Sergeant Montgomery. I'll be staying with you tonight." His hand was warm when he shook her hand. She felt the butterflies in her stomach begin to melt away. It would be alright. There was no way Riperton could reach any of them now. It was only a matter of time before he was caught.

Still, she lay in bed, wide awake until her cellphone chirruped. She snatched at it, glancing at her alarm, seeing a blue neon 1:02 am. Her fingers fumbled for the switch of the bedside lamp, and the light stabbed at her eyes in the darkness. She squinted at the phone's display. It showed Lauren's number. Why would Lauren call her at this time? "Lauren?"

Lauren's voice screamed in her ear. "Jesse! The

barn's on fire! Hurry!" Then she was gone.

The barn on fire! Jesse lunged out of bed, grabbed her jeans and boots, and bolted in her pajamas down the hall to her father's door. The hardwood floor echoed her bare feet. Her voice cracked when she yelled. "Dad! Dad! Wake up!" She pounded on his door. "The Saucier's barn is on fire!"

He flung open the door, already fastening jeans, a shirt in his hand. "Go get the police officer. I'll grab some ropes and halters. Meet you at the truck." He said, lips thin and grim.

He arrived at the truck, loaded with equipment, at the same time she did. Montgomery waited in the squad car out in the drive while they scrambled into the cab. The roar of the truck jarred the night, lurching and jumping as it shot down the driveway, police car following, while Jesse struggled to get her jeans over her pajamas. By the time they raced into Saucier's drive, she'd wrestled on her boots

From the truck, Jesse could smell the acrid stench of fire. Thick brown smoke billowed out the open barn doors while dim shapes rushed in and out. Bright orange tendrils of flame snaked out windows in the middle of the barn, arcing sparks up into the dark night sky. Her heart froze and for a moment she couldn't move. Starbuck's stall had been right there, in the middle of the barn. Lauren's silhouette led a horse away from the bright orange of the flames.

"Jesse!" Her father's voice snapped her panic as he shoved some ropes into her hands. She had to save Starbuck. She rushed forward, stopping at the doorway long enough to drop all but one of the ropes. As she plunged into the barn, she met Lauren's father on his way out. He led a giant bay Warmblood that wheeled frantic circles around him.

He said something to her, but the panicked cries of nearby horses and the cracking hissing fire muffled his voice. She shook her head at him and yelled, "I can't hear you! Where's Starbuck? Is he out yet?"

He hollered over his shoulder as the horse pulled him away, "He's okay, we got him and Legs out right away! Let your dad take the horses closest to the fire!"

She whirled to see her father disappear into the stall next to Starbuck's. Vivid flames pushed their way up the walls and into that stall. She breathed a silent prayer for him and started to run to one of the stalls further down the barn where the flames hadn't reached yet. But she stopped when she heard a shrill whinny from the stall across the alley from Legs' stall.

The flames had reached across the ceiling, sending fingers into several stalls on that side of the barn. She looked down the barn alley for help, but her father already had his horse headed toward the door. She couldn't see anyone else. If that horse didn't get rescued soon, it'd die trapped in that stall. She made up her mind and lunged across to the trapped horse's stall door. Inside, flames already licked the ceiling. The horse inside crouched low in the back, staring at her with wild fear-crazed eyes.

Jesse wrenched open the hot door and stepped in. The horse recoiled back against the wall. She stopped and held out one hand as if to offer it a treat. "Look. See, I have a treat for you. I know you're going to be a good horse and I have something for you."

The ceiling began to rain small ignited chunks into the woodchip bedding. The heat from above began to bear down on her, and she blinked the sting of the sweat from her eyes. Her pajama top clung to her back. She took another step and the horse glanced to either side of it for a way to run, but held its ground. Jesse inched forward and patted the horse on the shoulder with her fingertips. She slid her hand up the length of its wet neck and then reached over it to catch the end of the lead rope from her other hand.

The touch of the rope acted as an electric shock to the unnerved horse. It bolted toward the open stall door, knocking Jesse hard with its shoulder, and twisting her sideways and off balance. If not for the rope around the horse's neck, she would have gone down. As it was, the horse dragged her. As it tried to force its way through the stall door, the weight of the horse crushed Jesse's arm against the metal bracing and she gasped. A numb tingle reached her fingers. Then the horse jumped into the alley, and pulled her with it.

Jesse leaned all her weight against the horse's momentum, buckling her knees to lower her center of gravity. The horse reared and plunged. It shook its head, fighting against the weight on its neck. Her injured arm didn't let her hold onto the rope very well, and her other arm began to feel the stress of the extra weight against it.

Jesse leaned against the rope the whole way up the alley to the barn door, the horse's breath rasping in its throat. Her father ran back into the barn for another horse. He paused when he saw her. "Can you handle this one? If you can't, just let go."

Her arm still ached, but it didn't have that numbness anymore. And she was keeping to her feet better now. "I'm okay." He nodded and ran into the smoke again.

Once outside the barn, she saw shapes that became people. Other neighbors handled ropes and buckets of water. Ahead, Lauren led a horse toward the paddocks. As it danced around and around Lauren, Jesse could dimly see on its flank a big patch of raw burnt flesh surrounded by blackened hair. The thought of Starbuck sprang to her mind. She swallowed hard. Starbuck was okay. Barry had said so. She needed to focus that.

One of the neighbors held open the gate at the holding paddock and Jesse let her horse join the other horses that milled around the far side of the pen. Jesse climbed up on the cold metal rail, but didn't see her palomino anywhere. She raised herself up on tiptoe to spy on the other two pens.

"Jesse, he's in the third pen, the one by the woods. He's not hurt. I already checked," her father said, as he released another rescued horse into the pen. This one charged off kicking and squealing. Jesse turned toward the third pen just in time to see a golden head look over the top of the crowd, and then dip down out of sight again. Relief washed over her, and her eyes filled with tears. She blinked hard a few times to make them stop. She jumped down and her father squeezed her shoulder.

A loud crash came from the back of the barn, followed by terrified cries from the last of the horses trapped within the building. Jesse and her father rushed back into the barn. Jesse gulped in a huge swallow of smoke. She coughed and gagged, the smoke burning her nose and throat. Her eyes welled up with tears and refused to stay open more than a squint. Through the haze, she saw a handler who tried to lead another horse out, but the horse balked stiff-legged, jerking its handler back towards its stall. Jesse rushed beside the horse, flung her rope against its hip, and yelled savagely. The horse shot toward the barn door, almost knocking over its handler.

Still almost blind, Jesse whirled around to continue her way to the last horses. She didn't know how many remained, but they needed to be gotten out. Ahead, toward the back of the barn, lay a huge pile of debris burning against one side of the alley. Above it, smoke eddied into the sky. The crash she'd heard had been part of the roof. She just hoped all those horses escaped in time.

She heard a horse kick against its stall and hurried toward it. The gray jumper inside reared against the wall, striking its forefeet against the door again and again. She couldn't control this one. She'd have to chase it out and let it run. They would find it later. She pulled open the door and scrambled aside just as the horse bellowed past her, charging out of sight to the front of the barn. "Loose horse!" she yelled. Her voice shook and it didn't sound like hers anymore. The fire snapped closer.

Jesse raced to the next stall. Inside, Polly's mare leaned against one corner of the back wall. Smoke clouded a front corner of the stall, and the mare had backed as far away from it as she could. Jesse had always liked this horse and had fed it the occasional treat. She just hoped the little mare remembered her now. She voice soft, she said, "Hi, Sweetheart. Remember me? I'm the one who brings you all those wonderful nummies."

Bint Syrah trembled as she opened the door and came near, but didn't move. Jesse eased a halter over her nose and fastened the ear buckle. She patted the horse on the neck for reassurance, turned the Arabian toward the door, and braced herself for the mare to bolt. The horse stepped quietly beside Jesse and waited. Jesse smiled, patting her again on the neck. She said to the little mare, "Leave it to Polly to have a sensible horse."

She led the roan mare into the hallway. Flames spiked out of nearby stalls on either side of her now. The smoke swirled heavier than before. It tasted like oil in her mouth, making her cough. It obscured everything but Bint Syrah's stall and its neighbors. She turned first one way then the other, but she couldn't see the exit. The Arabian shuddered harder, leaning against her.

Jesse couldn't remember which side of the barn she'd been on. She twisted her head back and forth, trying to see through the wall of smoke, but she couldn't tell which way the exit lay. Her lungs burned with each gasp she took. The smoke pinched her nose and burned her drying eyes. Her head pounded. She wanted to collapse and lie down for a nap.

Then a thin wail pierced through the smoke. A fire truck. Bint Syrah heard it, too, and turned her head to the left, ears pricked toward the sound. Jesse smiled and coaxed the mare into a run, though she still couldn't see very far in front of them. At least now she knew which way to go. Flames leapt out of the wall at them as they ran. She smelled singed hair. She didn't know which one of them it belonged to, but didn't dare stop to find out. They dodged around a pile where the front of a stall had collapsed. The smoke thinned and Jesse could see that they'd almost reached the door. A fireman rushed toward her, her father right behind, a worried frown on his face. The fireman asked, "Are you all right miss?"

She nodded. "All the horses are out, I think. I didn't see any more."

"Yours is the last," her father said. "Are you sure you're all right?" He looked her up and down as if to reassure himself. He put his arm around her shoulder.

Jesse grinned and said, "I'm fine, a little smoky, but fine. Did we rescued them all? What happened to the police officer who was supposed to be watching the barns?"

"I don't know. No one's had time to look for him

yet. The horses are all safe. A few need the vet, but they'll heal."

Not a single horse had died. She remembered the horse Lauren had been leading and felt the need to see Starbuck. She'd go check on him just as soon as she put Polly's mare away. Then she'd get a very big glass of water.

Outside, fire hoses snaked across the ground, crossing lines with stretched garden hoses. Ropes and halters tangled with them. Horses whinnied in the background. Still in a panic, they kicked and fought. People rushed from the paddocks to the house, from the trucks and police cars to the barn. The fire growled and hissed behind them. Cars, trucks, fire trucks and an ambulance stood at odd angles and their red, blue and yellow emergency lights strobed across everything.

Polly's Arabian halted and stared wild-eyed, jerking her head first one direction, then another. Then she lunged backward, her hips low to the ground, backing as quickly as she could get her legs to move.

Jesse hurried to move with her. "Whoa girl. Easy." She spoke as low and as calm as she could. "Easy girl." As Jesse moved, she tried to circle to the side of the mare so she could pull her to a stop. The little horse pulled her deep into the brush beside the barn. Her father followed, cutting wide to get behind the horse. Jesse could hear the sounds of others who ran to help.

The rope slipped a few inches, and she renewed her grip. She glanced at the tail of the rope to make sure no loops would snag her hand. She'd seen people who'd lost fingers like that. The mare reared and struck out at her with her front feet. Then she lunged to the side, burning the rope through Jesse's hands. Jesse tried to hold on, but the rope slipped away. Bint Syrah crashed into the underbrush of the woods. Her father sprinted after the horse, joined by Barry Saucier and the few who had come to help.

Jesse stood a moment and watched them go. They would catch her. The mare wouldn't go far away from the other horses. The rope burn bit at her hands. She knew without looking that she'd lost some skin, but she was too tired to cry. Her parched throat needed a gallon of water. Maybe two. All she could smell was smoke. It had probably ruined her clothes. Her eyes burned like sandpaper, her lungs felt seared and raw, and she thought her head would explode. She turned around and started to push her way through the weeds and back to the house.

CHAPTER 24

The brush rustled behind Jesse. Had they caught Polly's horse already? She twisted around to see. The weeds crossed themselves in the night breeze, bowing and trembling. Shapes appeared and vanished in the glow from the fire. "Hello?" She asked, "Is anyone there?" The plants sighed against each other, rubbing leaves. She craned her neck, tiptoeing forward. Was that a person? "Hello?" Only the night answered her, and she shrugged, returning to her trek to the house.

Behind her, the brush crinkled and she glanced over her shoulder, unwilling to be fooled into turning all the way around again. She started to get that creepy feeling, like ants crawling on her body. The same wall of leaves stared at her. Nobody trudged behind her. Of course, nobody. She was way too tired and her imagination made her paranoid. She shook her head. What a freak.

She continued on her path. Shouldn't she be out of the weeds by now? She stopped and stood on tiptoe again. The barn burned to her left, parts of it only smoldering now. Not more than fifty feet ahead she could just make out the edge of the clearing.

Her foot bumped up against something hard, and she looked down. A lightening bolt of fear shot through her and her mouth went dry. She'd bumped into a person, lying on the ground. Hearing the brush behind her crinkle again, she whirled around. A shape pushed its way through the weeds and stood in front of her. In the dim light, she could see the hooked nose. Louis Riperton.

Jesse backed up, stepping over the person on the ground. Then she pivoted to run. Rough gasoline-smelling hands clamped her nose, mouth, and shoulder. Her stomach pitched within her. She wrenched herself back and forth, squirming to get her weight low enough that he couldn't hold her. She sucked in tiny puffs of gasoline-flavored air through his fingers.

A harsh whisper cut into her ear. "You think you're so smart, don't you? You think you saved your little horsey. Well, I'm gonna hurt him. I'm gonna hurt him real bad. Just as soon as I'm done with you. I'm gonna hurt you real bad, too. Just like this here police officer. I killed him. I'll kill you, too. You're gonna be real sorry you ever heard the names Louis Riperton or Mark Banks."

Not if Jesse could help it. She lifted her leg and cracked the heel of her boot as hard as she could against his shin. Riperton grunted and loosened his grip. Again and again she connected boot to bone with all the force she could muster. Then she made one more violent twist, and she broke free. She launched through the brush toward the house, the weeds tearing at her clothes and skin.

Riperton hissed from close behind her. "I'll catch you! You can't outrun me!"

Jesse pushed every ounce of energy she could find into her legs. If she could just make the clearing, someone would be there to help her. She heard Riperton crash through the brush right behind her, imagining his hands reaching closer and closer. She could almost smell the gasoline. Where was that clearing?

The vegetation fell away before her and she rocketed into the open. People. Cars. Flashing lights. Safety. A glance behind her told her that Riperton still chased close behind. He looked determined. And angry. He had his knife.

She saw her father outlined by the glow of the fire, standing by the house with a small group of people around Polly's mare. She yelled as loud as she could. "Dad! Help! Dad!" Would he hear her? Would he get to her in time? Tears sprang into her eyes and she yelled again. "Dad! Dad! Help me! Dad!"

He must have heard her that time. He whipped around and dropped the mare's lead, sprinting toward her. She glanced behind her again. Riperton followed her not more than a few steps away. She could hear his gasps for air.

She looked back at her father. Mr. Saucier and a third man had joined the chase. But they were still so far away. Even if they met her halfway, she'd never make it to them before Riperton caught her. The holding paddocks were closer. She could hide with the horses. She changed direction. Riperton followed.

She reached the third paddock and skinnied between the rails. The cool metal brushed against her sweaty back, sending a chill up her spine. Riperton's hand brushed against her leg just as she squeezed through. He tried to wedge between the bars after her, but his chest wouldn't fit. He jerked back and began to climb, clanging his knife against the paddock with every fresh handgrip.

Jesse stood almost in the middle of the pen. She'd

be safe if she stayed in that spot. The horses crowded at the far side of the enclosure. She lunged at them, waving her arms and screaming. They scattered to race around the paddock, their hooves rumbling the ground like a train. They circled around behind her and then shied straight across the other side of the pen when they saw the shape of a man standing on the railing. Jesse stepped back a little to give them room. Between their bodies, Jesse could see snatches of the shadow that was her father as he ran closer.

Louis Riperton shifted his head back and forth between Jesse and her father. Slowly, he eased down into the pen. The horses moved that side of their circle farther away from him and closer to Jesse. That gave her an idea. Maybe she could force Riperton back out of the pen by pushing the circle closer to him. She stepped toward him, her arms above her head. It worked. The horses shifted that side of their circle away from her, toward Riperton again. She took another step.

Riperton raised his arms in a mimic of her. He took a step toward her. The horses hesitated and snorted with their noses high the air. Jesse jumped back to give the horses room to run between them, but a gap had opened up. Riperton dove across it. He rolled into the middle of the pen with her and the horses resumed their frantic pace around the two of them. Jesse searched for her father. He had reached the side of the paddock with the two other shadows. The same circle of horses that had kept her attacker away now kept her locked into the middle with him. She was trapped, and her rescuers couldn't get to her.

The moon ducked behind a cloud, and edged the pen into darkness. Jesse could almost hear Riperton breathe above the noise of the hooves. She started to edge toward her father, but Riperton circled around in the way. She couldn't open a gap in the horses for her father without moving closer to Riperton. Her heart froze.

A flash of gold circled behind Riperton. Starbuck! If she could get on him and make him circle with the others, she could get away. She could push him across the stream of horses while they all circled. Then when she got close enough to the rail and her father, she could jump off.

She jumped straight sideways toward the course of horses, cutting off Starbuck's path. She held her left arm out to the side. "Whoa!" The nearest horses shot around anyway, but Starbuck and several others stopped. Confused, a couple of the horses behind pivoted and began to circle in the opposite direction. As they met other horses, those squealed and kicked. The circle broke into a milieu. Starbuck held his ground. Jesse ran up to his side, jump-scrambling onto his wide back. Hot sweat soaked up into her jeans.

Riperton had closed the ground between them and now clamped an iron hand around her ankle. Mean eyes glared up at her. "You're pretty smart, but not as smart as me. Now I'm gonna hurt you and your horse." He sneered and lowered his knife toward Starbucks belly.

Jesse leaned forward and away from her attacker, bringing her trapped leg in toward herself. Then she shoved her foot into his chest with all her might. A loud "whuf!" came from Riperton and he stumbled back, dropping the knife. He started to fall, but used his grip on her leg to pull himself upright again. She slammed her other heel into Starbuck's flank. "Please, Starbuck. Remember your lessons," she whispered. If he would just move his hip, that would push him even further into her attacker. It might be enough to get Riperton to let go. If he didn't remember the Turn on the Forehand, and decided to go forward, Riperton would unseat her.

Starbuck waggled his ears back and forth. Then he began to shift his weight. Jesse could feel him pick up his hind foot and step toward Riperton.

"Good boy! Go, go, go, go, go!" Jesse bumped him harder and faster with her heel, nagging him to move faster. Starbuck took another step. Then another and another.

Riperton stumbled backwards. Each time he regained his balance, Starbuck bumped him again. Jesse kept her other heel against Starbuck's flank like a staccato rhythm. She pulled in her pinned leg one more time. The next time Starbuck bumped against Riperton, she punched her leg into her attackers chest again.

Riperton fell, but he took Jesse with him. She ripped out some of Starbuck's mane as she fell. Riperson wrenched her leg when he didn't let go. His fingernails dug into her jeans and bit through to her skin underneath. She twisted around on the ground and kicked whatever she could reach until he let go. Then she scrambled backward as fast as she could. Starbuck snorted and bolted away to join the other horses.

Then Detective Lowrey was there. He kneeled beside Riperton with one knee on his back, putting on handcuffs. Jesse's father rushed over to her and wrapped his arms around her. He held her tight and whispered, "It's over. It's all over."

CHAPTER 25

The next morning, Jesse sighed and scuffed at a pile of sopping ashes. This was where the tack room had been. All her tack had been here: her reclaimed Stubben, her bridles and all her equipment. The only thing she had left at her home was her old jumping saddle. She squinted her eyes, and searched for where Starbuck's stall had been. The early morning light glinted from dark spires of charred timber, sharpening the burnt edges. Occasional smoke still spiraled up from the mounds of embers. A darker black showed the only evidence that Starbuck's stall had ever existed.

Riperton had almost gotten them both. Not just them, either, but all the other horses, and her friends, too. Detective Lowrey had told her that Riperton had been denied bond. He was going to be there a very long time. He'd been booked on Theft, Arson, Assault, Attempted kidnapping, Attempted Murder, and Murder. And Starbuck had broken Riperton's ankle.

The screen door to Lauren's house banged, and Jesse left her thoughts to see her friend clump down the porch stairs, waving at her. "The vet will be here soon." she called in a scratchy voice. Jesse nodded and joined her, walking toward the paddocks. Her own voice wasn't much better. Neither one of them had gotten much sleep. They drug their boots through the black mud in time together.

Lauren snorted and said, "I couldn't eat my breakfast. It smelled like smoke."

Jesses answered. "I know, everything I smell and taste is that way."

"How long do you think it'll be like that?"

"Couple days, I guess."

"When do you take your algebra test?"

"Dad's gonna reschedule it again. He doesn't think I can concentrate well enough on it yet. I think he's right."

Lauren didn't say anything as they climbed the rails of the paddock Legs stood in. Bint Syrah limped alongside the far rail. A full half of the mare's tail had burned, and one of her hocks puffed with blisters all over it. "So that's the hair I smelled burning."

"Dad says it looks worse than it really is. Just a few blisters. She had a burnt cinder wedged in her frog, but she'll recover." Lauren frowned.

Jesse frowned, too. Her frog. That could mean trouble, if it didn't heal right. Polly could be grounded for a while. She might miss a few competitions. "You think her tail will come back in white?"

"I dunno. It'd be cool, though, if it did."

Jesse shuffled her feet on the rail, twisting to sit on the top rail. She faced the burn. The brush had been burned in a wide swathe around the barn area. Dark paths where the fire had sent fingers twisted through the weeds. "Dad says we can bring Legs and one more down to our house with Starbuck."

Lauren scooted to sit next to Jesse, leaning over to crush her in a hug. "I don't know what I'd do if I had to

161

send her to another stable where I couldn't see her every day. Thanks."

"I'm gonna get Starbuck freezebranded."

Lauren nodded and they sat side by side in silence until a single shrill cry from a passing bird pierced the air. Then Jesse said, "I feel like this is all my fault. I mean Riperton wouldn't have burned the barn if it hadn't been for Starbuck and me."

"Yeah, you're right. Instead, he probably would have burned it when he broke in to steal our stuff, too. Goof!" Lauren stuck out her tongue and made a face. Jesse laughed and it felt good. Lauren said, "Dad's already talked to the insurance company. They're gonna pay for all the tack that burned up. That means everyone gets new saddles." She grinned at Jesse.

"And new bridles?"

"Yep. And new brushes."

"New halters and ropes?"

"And new picture frames."

"New what?"

Lauren wagged her finger at Jesse. "I kept a picture of Legs in my tack box. Don't tell me you didn't keep one of Starbuck in yours."

"Well, yeah." Jesse shrugged.

"So?"

"And we get new picture frames."

"Exactly."

Jesse smiled. "And a new barn."

"Only better. Dad's gonna add a covered arena."

Jesse swiveled to stare at Lauren, who sat up straighter. "Really?"

"M-hmm. It'll be big enough to jump in." Lauren's eyes sparkled. "And it'll have six more stalls. It'll be ginormous!"

"No more mud."

"Or rain."

"No more wind."

"No more snow."

Jesse shook her head, her mouth open. She couldn't even picture it. She turned back to stare at the black space, trying to place a bigger barn there, one with a covered arena attached. An oily-smoky haze had begun to rise, hugging close to the ground. When she squinted her eyes, she could almost see the new barn sitting in the middle of it.

Lauren broke into her thoughts. "We'll school year round and stop missing the early spring shows. Hey! We can even have our own schooling shows during the winter!"

Jesse grinned at Lauren and said, "I don't know how to organize a show, but I'll bet it's fun."

"Do you know what's going to happen to Stacey's horses?"

"Nope, but Detective Lowrey said we could keep Kula and her baby, when it's born, with grampa until they decide what to do with her. I'm going to see if I can keep her permanently."

"Really? That would be too cool." Lauren nodded just as the veterinarian pulled into the driveway, followed closely by Haley's green and brown bronco. Lauren nudged her and whispered, "I think she likes your dad."

"Really? You think so?"

"Yeah, who do you think called her?" They watched the woman knock on the door of Lauren's house and then enter. "I think he likes her, too."

"That wouldn't be too bad."

"Nope." Then Lauren stood, pivoting on the rail to watch her horse again. She said to Jesse, not turning her head, "Next year, at the Aroostook Classic, I'm gonna stomp you."

Jesse stood and looked over to the third paddock. Starbuck stood in what little sunrays he could find unoccupied, his head down and hip cocked. His soft gold coat still had smudges of smoke streaked across it, and his long, long almost white tail had taken on a definite brown tint. He looked scraggly and filthy. She'd always thought he was prettier than any other horse. Today he looked perfect. She smiled and turned to Lauren. "I don't think so."

THE END